THE LEGACY SERIES

SERIES TITLES

Apple & Palm
Patricia Henley

Bodies in Bags
Jamey Gallagher

A Green Glow on the Horizon
Dawn Burns

How We Do Things Here
Matt Cashion

Neon Steel
Jennifer Maritza McCauley

Release of Information
Kali White VanBaale

The Divide
Evan Morgan Williams

Yes, No, I Don't Know
Kathryn Gahl

The Price of Their Toys
John Loonam

The Caged Man
Calvin Mills

A Day Doesn't Go By When I Don't Have Regrets
J. Malcolm Garcia

These Are My People
Steve Fox

We Should Be Somewhere by Now
Stephen Tuttle

Burner and Other Stories
Katrina Denza

The Plan of Chicago
Barry Pearce

Trust Issues
K.P. Davis

Adult Children
Laurence Klavan

Guardians & Saints
Diane Josefowicz

Western Terminus: Stories and A Novella
Michael Keefe

Like Human
Janet Goldberg

The Hopefuls
Elizabeth Oness

Never Stop Exiting
Michael Hopkins

Broken Heart Syndrome
Anne Colwell

The Mexican Messiah: A Novella & Stories
Jay Kauffmann

Close to a Flame
Colleen Alles

American Animism
Jamey Gallagher

Keeping What's Best Left Kept Secret
David Ricchiute

Soaked
Toby LeBlanc

The Path of Totality
Marie Zhuikov

Shocker in Gloomtown
Dan Libman

The Continental Divide
Bob Johnson

The Three Devils and Other Stories
William Luvaas

The Correct Response
Manfred Gabriel

Welcome Back to the World: A Novella & Stories
Rob Davidson

Greyhound Cowboy and Other Stories
Ken Post

Close Call
Kim Suhr

The Waterman
Gary Schanbacher

Signs of the Imminent Apocalypse and Other Stories
Heidi Bell

What We Might Become
Sara Reish Desmond

The Silver State Stories
Michael Darcher

An Instinct for Movement
Michael Mattes

The Machine We Trust
Tim Conrad

Gridlock
Brett Biebel

Salt Folk
Ryan Habermeyer

The Commission of Inquiry
Patrick Nevins

Maximum Speed
Kevin Clouther

Reach Her in This Light
Jane Curtis

The Spirit in My Shoes
John Michael Cummings

The Effects of Urban Renewal on Mid-Century America and Other Crime Stories
Jeff Esterholm

What Makes You Think You're Supposed to Feel Better
Jody Hobbs Hesler

Fugitive Daydreams
Leah McCormack

Hoist House: A Novella & Stories
Jenny Robertson

Finding the Bones: Stories & A Novella
Nikki Kallio

Self-Defense
Corey Mertes

Where Are Your People From?
James B. De Monte

Sometimes Creek
Steve Fox

The Plagues
Joe Baumann

The Clayfields
Elise Gregory

Kind of Blue
Christopher Chambers

Evangelina Everyday
Dawn Burns

Township
Jamie Lyn Smith

Responsible Adults
Patricia Ann McNair

Great Escapes from Detroit
Joseph O'Malley

Nothing to Lose
Kim Suhr

The Appointed Hour
Susanne Davis

PRAISE FOR
Apple & Palm

Henley's stirring collection follows characters navigating shifting relationships and pivotal moments in their lives. . . . Focused largely on women, Henley's tales remain finely attuned to the characters' discomforts, desires, and moments of revelation amidst social expectations.

—*BOOKLIST*

Henley is . . . a Mistress of the short story craft and her mastery of the genre not only glistens, it tugs at heart and mind. *Apple & Palm*—a literal intersection in Whistle Pig—is a place that defies pervasive stereotypes that typecast rural Americans as less educated and more conservative than their urban counterparts....Flawed but fully human, [her characters] both inspire and entertain.

—*TURNED PAGE REVIEW*

There is such tenderness and grace in Patricia Henley's exquisite new collection *Apple & Palm*, where each story, rich with detail, captures the delicate passage of time and the ephemeral nature of youth. Subtle, nuanced, and masterfully told, these stories will leave you quietly devastated and profoundly moved.

—ANDREW PORTER
author of *The Imagined Life*

We have all stood at the intersection of *Apple & Palm*, but only Patricia Henley could deliver such involving, heartening, memorable stories about what happened there and beyond. I loved this collection.

—JO-ANN MAPSON
author of *The Return of Lindsay Moon*

These deeply atmospheric, sensuous, richly textured stories have a Winesburgian feel. We quickly grow close to Henley's intricately connected ensemble of brave, striving women as they give their essences—across eras, and vividly drawn landscapes—to make sense of their difficult worlds, struggling to transcend (or make uneasy peace with) what is given—and what is taken away. Wonderfully imagined and compassionately told, *Apple and Palm* acts like a dark mirror: it holds our gaze.

—JOAN FRANK
author of *Juniper Street*

Patricia Henley burrows deeply into the hearts and minds of her characters. A salty, earned wisdom pervades *Apple & Palm*. Nothing is clean-cut or predictable; life is suitably messy. But, oh, do the sentences sing! These linked stories explore aging, memory, and desire amidst a refreshingly diverse range of sexual orientations. The urgency in these pages is both palpable and eloquent. A masterful collection that will surprise and charm the reader.

—ROB DAVIDSON
author of *Welcome Back to the World*

Apple
&
Palm

stories

Patricia Henley

CORNERSTONE PRESS
UNIVERSITY OF WISCONSIN-STEVENS POINT

Cornerstone Press, Stevens Point, Wisconsin 54481
Copyright © 2026 Patricia Henley
www.uwsp.edu/cornerstone

Printed in the United States of America.

Library of Congress Control Number: 2026930354
ISBN: 978-1-968148-21-8

All rights reserved.

This is a work of fiction. Names, characters, businesses, places, events, and incidents are either the products of the author's imagination or used in a fictitious manner. Any resemblance to actual persons, living or dead, or actual events is purely coincidental.

Cornerstone Press titles are produced in courses and internships offered by the Department of English at the University of Wisconsin–Stevens Point.

DIRECTOR & PUBLISHER	EXECUTIVE EDITORS
Dr. Ross K. Tangedal	Jeff Snowbarger, Freesia McKee
EDITORIAL DIRECTOR	SENIOR EDITORS
Brett Hill	Lhea Owens, Paige Biever, Ellie Atkinson

PRESS STAFF
Samantha Bjork, Sophie McPherson, Andrew Bryant, Eleanor Belcher, Gwen Goetter, Brian Grzesik, Kimberly Janesch, Ryleigh Miller, Sam Zajkowski

for Gaye Berryman, lifelong friend

ALSO BY PATRICIA HENLEY:

FICTION
Other Heartbreaks
In the River Sweet
Worship of the Common Heart
Hummingbird House
The Secret of Cartwheels
Friday Night At Silver Star

POETRY
Back Roads
Learning to Die

STORIES

Currency   1

Apple & Palm   23

What Goes Around   46

Truer Words   73

Smorgasbord   92

Sally's Tangent   104

Pivot   121

Kokoro   139

Acknowledgments   155

*How much better is silence; the coffee cup, the table.
How much better to sit by myself like the solitary
sea-bird that opens its wings on the stake. Let me sit here
forever with bare things, this coffee cup, this knife, this
fork, things in themselves, myself being myself.*

—Virginia Woolf

Currency

Roxy McAuliffe inhabits the back house on the alley, once a garage, what people now call a studio, with its miniature kitchen, concrete floor, and tiny windows with their decomposing putty. She can't manage the craggy front steps up to the Tansy anymore. Tansy Art Dispensary. A place for women artists to live and sell their work. Her framed, sepia-tone photographs hang in the gallery. She sold enough to supplement working at the shirt factory, and later, when the shirt factory closed, she worked part-time at the public library. Not that she absolutely needed the money—Joe Bosko made sure of that. But she loved the work routines. Now she crumbles from within. Crumbling bones will be her demise.

She had an affair with a much older man years ago. Her last affair. He worked at a photography store in Cumberland. She was a month shy of forty, a single mother with a six-year-old, in what's now called a green-card marriage. A developer of film, when she came in to buy supplies, he would emerge from the darkroom as if he'd just woken up, blinking and blinking; they had talked a little, enough for her to know that he went to a Zen meditation group, a novelty in those days, but she suspects that now there are Zen meditation groups in almost every scruffy small town. How did he know that she was in the store? Perhaps the woman who worked the front alerted him. One thing led to another and before long she was spending one night a week in his apartment over the store. For decades, Tansy residents have come in handy as babysitters. What she remembers most of the time she spent with him is feeling free. Free to walk around the room at least half naked. Free to let him know what she wanted. Once she asked him about the difference between being his age and being her age. He said, "I live in memory more."

That was sixty years ago. Now she lives in memory, too. Memory like a museum. Fusty. Bestrewn with YouTube videos.

Her grandson, Norman, calls her a super-centenarian. At one time, before she got pregnant with Norman's mother, she might have been called a spinster.

Norman's wife, Lulu, decides that she's more a thornback. Thornbacks, she says, are powerful women who never marry, as if her marriage of convenience to Mike Bosko never happened. As if pretending to get married when the war in Europe ended, that windy night on the beach in Queensland, never happened. Spinster connotes a dried-up woman with no memory of walking naked around the room in front of her lover, someone with a rosary in her lap and a penchant for African violets. "I see you with a thornback tat," Lulu teases, "if you were the tat sort." Roxy suspects that Lulu herself rues the day she married Norman. Marriage has a way of diminishing some women. Years ago, she might have said most women, but she has learned to temper her pronouncements.

Lulu calls before six in the morning. They are friends, as well as in-laws, and they long ago established that it's okay to call anytime. Roxy has been up before the birds. "Change, change," Lulu says, "is in the air." A spurt of excitement jolts

Roxy's veins when she realizes that Lulu is coming to see her without Norman.

Norman makes everything about himself. He bosses Lulu and the children. He talks about his art, his sales. He's told her three times that the mayor of Harpers Ferry purchased one of his paintings. This is to justify gouging her for money for art supplies. But when Lulu comes alone, or with the children, anything could happen.

There might be dancing. The hokey pokey. Laughter. Confidences that expose Roxy and Lulu to a raw intimacy. A miracle, at her age. They have told each other about the first time they had sex, about their most humiliating moments. Roxy has seen Lulu's stretch marks, like zebra stripes across her tanned belly and breasts. Once a year, Lulu checks Roxy over, all over, for moles, to determine whether she needs a visit to the dermatologist.

The baby on her hip, Lulu rushes into the back house, wearing a magenta scarf around her forehead: she always manages to impart an earthy—dare Roxy use the word tribal?—fashion sense. How does she know that Lulu might not be contented with Norman? She conveys this with glances that sweep toward Roxy under Norman's radar. She loves her to pieces, as people used to say. Sometimes she's not sure if what people used to say is common anymore. Surely no one says, "Hold your horses," but Roxy finds it right on the tip of her tongue. It's odd to be over one hundred years old and still functioning in this different world. She doesn't want to say the wrong thing. She wants to use the right pronouns. She doesn't want to be scorned or laughed at, even now. She doesn't want to hurt anyone. She wants to keep those secrets coming.

Lately, she rehearses begging Lulu not to leave Norman and move back to West Virginia, where her mama has a bed-and-cocktail, she calls it, in a former mining town. Lulu's mama was a miner, one of the first women miners. Lulu was supposedly conceived in the mine; it's her mama's personal legend. Her arm was chewed up in an accident and she quit mining to run the bed-and-cocktail. Lulu probably feels as if her life story is slight compared to her mama's; that may be why she dresses in outlandish clothes; that may be why she curses a blue streak. To take up space. The name of the mining town sometimes falls behind the wall in Roxy's brain. The wall is freckled with straw. She loses the names of the simplest things back there—an eggbeater, an antihistamine. Or the name of a neighbor or a flower. She never tells anyone about the wall. When would she ever see Lulu again if she went home to her mama? Lulu and the children are her lifeline to the larger world, her salve, her *joie de vivre*. Sometimes she realizes she has said this thing out loud to Lulu one way or the other. Don't leave the area without telling me first. What would I do without you?

The pregnancy test is in the pocket of Lulu's dress. She pats the pocket tentatively, as if testing an iron for heat. Then, like a shaman, she lifts out the test and shakes the box so that her bracelets rattle. She hands Roxy the baby—they call her Toots—and goes into the bathroom. She has dropped the boy, Nate, at kindergarten, only a block away.

The baby squirms to get down. She's ready to be on her own already, grinning and squeezing the corduroy of the sofa cushion tight until she's stable on her plump legs. Then she plops to the floor. She accepts it. Roxy can see her deciding that crawling will suffice. She scrambles to a trio of pots and lids left out on the floor just for her. Lulu wails in the bathroom, and Toots bangs a lid on a pot. Lulu wails as if something heavy had fallen on her; she wails as if for help. She wails as if for her mama.

Lulu likes to change up Roxy's music. It keeps you young, she says. On YouTube she finds grainy clips (she calls them) of young people dancing to Glenn Miller and Tommy Dorsey. The dancers appear nearly boneless and confident: the boys flipping the girls over their backs and the girls flipping their skirts. They wore ankle socks with sensible shoes. The music clears away the cobwebs and memories emerge more fully formed. Ain't she sweet—a favorite. Ain't she sweet takes her back to Aunt Marsha, a teacher in a country town north of Sydney. Teachers were supposed to conform to common-denominator decorum laid down by Scots Irish congregations. But after their meager tea, Aunt Marsha would find a staticky radio station that played popular music for twenty minutes every evening except Sunday. They didn't have a rug to roll up. They danced on the worn lino. It was plain as plain could be. The cheapest. Big cabbage roses. They would dance until they were out of breath. Aunt Marsha would make her a hot cocoa and pour herself an inch of whiskey from a bottle she kept among the cleaning supplies behind the curtain under the sink.

Aunt Marsha taught her that women could drink and dance and still hold their heads up high.

In 1915, Roxy McAuliffe was born on a sheep station in New South Wales so remote that, at first, her mother was her teacher. After a few years, they sent her to live with Aunt Marsha, her mother's sister, a girl teacher, untrained, but she knew enough to get them through long division and Charles Dickens. Roxy longed for secretarial school and moved to Sydney as soon as they would let her. That's where she was living when her mother wrote to her, enclosing a black-and-white photograph, to say that her father had no choice but to destroy his sheep. During the Depression there was no market for wool.

In the photograph he's sitting in the dim kitchen, his knees splayed out, his khaki pants and flannelette shirt splattered with sheep's blood. They had dug a trench for burial, backed truck after truck full of sheep near the trench, and he had shot them one by one as they came off the tailgate. This went on for one long day. He hadn't the awareness to know that her mother was photographing him. She had an urge to photograph workers. A station hand from Spain had set up a makeshift darkroom in a root cellar and shown her how to develop her own prints. He went off and forgot one of his cameras and her mother claimed it for herself. Now Roxy realizes that the station hand must have given her mother the camera, but such a gift might have been suspect at the time. Her "minnie" she called the camera. Miniature. Workers—station hands, horse trainers—were the people of her world. In the photo, Roxy's father was stunned, a handkerchief to his sweaty face, weeping.

In that same letter, her mother sent her money to buy a camera. "Your life will surprise you," she wrote. "Keep a record of it."

All her life Roxy has photographed the natural world, but she has never grown accustomed to the puffy green mountains of Appalachia, her home since 1945. Recollections of the sheep station in New South Wales still occupy her, the curving hills, the gum trees, their medicinal scent in the dewy morning air, the windmill and its creak, the maggies chattering harshly to each other, a gargle deep in their shiny black throats. You get imprinted with images from babyhood. Most people long to return to childish astonishment. That's her theory, anyway. If they still have their wits about them, super-centenarians have loads of theories. Once Roxy found her way to Maryland, she rarely thought of leaving. Australia is so far.

She had enlisted in the Australian Women's Army Service on May 11, 1943, at Neutral Bay. Her rank was gunner. The girls who didn't go into the service probably regretted it. It was the grandest time. Stationed at Townsville, she lucked into a job driving a CO around and running errands. Freedom was hers, to a certain extent. That's how she met Leo Bosko, a Yank. She was told to fetch him and bring him to the site of a radio signal meeting between Aussies and Yanks. From that day onward, they had a special feeling for each other. They recognized each other from afar the next day, and the next. They held hands when they could, until they had a private walk along The Strand, where they declared themselves sweethearts. That's how she thought of it. The other girls razzed her without mercy. All the Australian girls wanted Yanks. They were a novelty. Roxy hadn't even wanted one, yet there was Leo, young, only twenty-two, strong, handsome, with black hair and dimples when he smiled. Wondrous lost inhibition comes with love, if you're fortunate, and lost inhibition is what she recalls of being with Leo. They would walk away from war. The coastal sunset would be broken up with gunmetal clouds crusted in orange. They discovered an old fish camp—a lean-to—near an estuary. Evening after evening, when they could arrange to be away, they added to the comfort there. An army green blanket. A lumpen feather pillow. A bedsheet. An ammo box containing a bottle of Bundy that scorched her chest going down.

I'll be seeing you in all the old familiar places that this heart of mine embraces all day through all day through all day through.
 "Who *is* that," she says to Lulu. The name has slipped behind the wall. A void she doesn't want to fall into.
 "Norah Jones. You remember Norah Jones. We've listened to this before."
 There is a neighbor, an old man, an elderly man, Lulu corrects her, who comes to her screen door and leans on his walker and listens. He is the kind of man who still takes care of himself. Lulu says that he probably uses a little battery-operated thingamajig to clip his nose hairs. He keeps his shoes polished, the lenses of his spectacles clean. The old man is alone in the alley of his life. And she is alone in the

back house of her life. Never again would she fall in love, travel long distances, live among a boisterous gaggle of women. Oh, the women of the Tansy come one by one to see her, taking turns bringing her supper every night. The back house isn't meant for a crowd. She has a single bed, a television, a loveseat, and the tiniest bathroom imaginable, with just enough room for her and her walker. She still wipes herself, but she needs help to take a shower. She never wants to become the sort of old lady who forgets how good it feels to be clean.

Her realm has shrunk, no getting around that. It started when she was seventy-nine and continued apace ever since, until one night at the kitchen table she told them that she needed to move to the back house where Lulu could drive right up to the door on the alley when she took her out.

Lulu says that the old man has a crush on her. That is the last thing she wants, a man sleeping over, taking up room in the already-too-small bed, pissing in her bathroom, dribbling on the rim, leaving up the toilet seat. Oh, there are geriatric couples in Whistle Pig. Lulu says they are adorbs. "My ass," Roxy thinks.

In fact, when she still lived in the Tansy, she never liked for a man to use the bathroom. If one did, a guest, a workman, whoever, she would grab a pail of cleaning supplies and hustle to the bathroom he had used and wipe everything down. Children, boy children, had to be accepted, but grown men—never.

Sometimes Lulu takes her to the senior center where there is a social director. She likes game night, playing double rummy, placing silly bets, macaroni pieces. They don't trust them to use real money. When the social director gathers everyone together to bat a balloon around a tabletop with pool noodles, a game for idiots, Roxy asks for Lulu and she comes to fetch her. The social director is one of those women for whom holiday decorations are necessary. For Halloween she puts up door-size posters of ghouls with witchy hair and

open toothless mouths. A life-size skeleton of plastic bones hangs just close enough to the dining room door that almost everyone rattles it coming to lunch. "It seems insensitive," Lulu says. So many elders, so close to dying. But Lulu is quick to say, "Oh, not you, Rox. You're spunky."
Lulu searches her iPad for "In the Mood."
Never felt so happy so fully alive jammin' jumpin' . . .
Oh, they were always in the mood.

Lulu bestows a seductive smile upon her to let her know that she understands being in the mood. As if Roxy couldn't tell. She's had two babies and there's another on the way.

When Toots falls asleep at the breast, Lulu says, "I. Just. Can't."

"What goes through your mind when you think about it?"

"Norman. He'll own me."

Roxy keeps this thought to herself: She never imagined she and Norman would ever be on the same side, wanting to keep Lulu restrained.

Roxy and Leo were stationed in Townsville on the northeast coast of Australia, a town attacked three times by the Japanese. Still, life has a way of going on, Leo would tell Roxy. They couldn't—shouldn't—put things on hold.

During the war, Ella Flynn had come out to Townsville to help her daughter care for her deaf boy. The daughter worked in a pub and Ella stayed with the boy, who was four years old. They were waiting until they had the money to send him away to Brisbane to a school for the deaf. They had two coffee cans, one for the money and one in which they accumulated bacon grease for future use. Ella was in her sixties; her life had taken the sort of turns that made her wish ill on people. Some people triumph over circumstance by singing hymns while they work or saying the rosary. Some, like Ella Flynn, have a homing instinct for occasions to hurt others. She longed to correct all their faults and mistakes; she thought people in general were liars and cheats. She had gone to Catholic school at a time when the nuns were repressed and taught meanness themselves. It's different now; then, certain women did not question instruction to be stingy with affection and delight. But she could put on a good front, especially to make money. A seamstress, during her apprenticeship in Brisbane she had acquired a papier-mâché and plaster mannequin. It could be adjusted to the proportions of any client, within reason. Ella had coated the sections with casein glue. She paid a digger to haul it to Townsville, and she determined to make dresses for the girls who were stationed there. Roxy learned all this over time. Ella Flynn was a talker once you got her started.

In 1944, dress material was in short supply. She had brought old dresses from Brisbane that she painstakingly ripped the seams from, washed, ironed, and folded into sheaves of what she told clients was like-new chiffon, gingham, and silk. "Like new, like new," she would repeat. A booklet she'd gotten from a sewing machine company gave instructions on how to turn men's suits into women's suits. Before she left Brisbane, she went around to houses where she knew men had lived who died in the war and she offered to buy the old clothes. She practiced and knew how to take a boxy tuxedo jacket and make it trim and fitted for a woman. And some of the girls had people in the States who sent them material for dresses. "It's quality," she would say of her own material, hoping to sell them more than one item. "Ah, ye want quality, don't ye?" The girls craved something new. They would go to dances with the Yanks or to the picture shows. Some of them were military. Some were civilians and worked during the day at the pink stucco Stafford Hotel, which had become the Australian Officer's Club. At night they went out in their new dresses and flirted with the Yanks, and Ella Flynn did not approve. But she wanted the money.

Leo's mother had sent Roxy three yards of dress material purchased at Rosenbaum Brothers Department Store in Cumberland, Maryland, over 9000 miles away. Sometimes, even now, if Norman takes her out to cash a check, Roxy likes to go by what used to be the magnificent Rosenbaum Department Store, with its red sandstone facade and lion's head medallions. Her entire life seems to have started there, unbeknownst to her, when Leo's mother went to the basement level and purchased three yards of fabric.

Roxy had heard about Ella Flynn from her daughter who worked at the Everyman and Everywoman. Leo and Roxy would go there for a cup of tea on the rooftop terrace. They might have been to the show and then played table tennis at the Y, and then to the Everyman and Everywoman. They made the tea strong; there would usually be a little sugar. Someone might have a bottle of native rum and Leo might prefer that, in Coke. Ella Flynn's daughter overheard them discussing the dress material and said, "My mum can make a dress for you. She's good at it." She gave directions to her house.

Roxy walked out on The Strand, the beach, way past their trysting spot, to where the walkway ended and the footpath began, in her regulation Army shoes, with their regulation one-inch heels. Her ankle socks slipped down and sand got in her shoes. She shaded her eyes with one hand. Sunlight glittered on the sand and on the sea. It beat down on her. Lunch hour was not the best time to be walking in the sun, but she wanted a new dress to wear for Leo. She carried a canvas haversack with the flowered rayon material inside. Sprigs of violets on a yellow background. In the barracks, the night before, the girls had played "You Made Me Love You" over and over. Surrendering to love was something they teased each other about. Lots of girls had decided to stay in Sydney. Their lives sounded drab. The girls who enlisted were having the time of their lives, and Roxy was old enough to know it. She was thirty, older than most of the other girls—older, but not wiser, for she had fallen in love with a much younger Yank.

Ella Flynn, the seamstress, and her daughter had rescued a ramshackle building left by an evacuee when Japan attacked. A section of the exterior still bore the sooty smears of a guinea grass fire. They made it into a makeshift home with a rustic charm, the door painted light coral and set amidst palm trees against a stony outcrop. An electrical wire that might have been illegal hung low behind the house. With one hip, Ella Flynn propped open the screen door and said, "So I hear ye got some dress material, lucky gal."

Roxy said yes and went inside with relief. Ella Flynn offered her a glass of water, which she accepted. The scanty dwelling was one room with bunk beds for the boy and his mother, and a rollaway cot acquired from a hotel for Ella Flynn. Shutters were closed against the sunlight; a table fan with one blade missing whirred on a windowsill. On a card table there was a jar of honey and a few slim bottles of condiments, some of which Roxy had not seen since 1941. The place smelled of wet wool like a wet dog. The wringer washer chugged at the sink and nearby lay piles of men's wool suits. Dead men's suits. The boy was still in his pajamas, with oatmeal smeared on his chin and his red hair, red like his mother's, sticking up in back like a rooster's comb. Ella Flynn said, "We're saving money to send him to Brisbane to the deaf school." That gave her a virtuous sheen. It said that the money Roxy spent on the dress would go to a good cause. The boy lay down on the bottom bunk bed and acted out battle with lead soldiers.

Ella Flynn had a treadle Singer sewing machine. An entire dining room table had been given over to the dressmaking: pinking shears and shoeboxes of thread and rickrack, patterns, a palm-size gingham pincushion in the shape of a rabbit. Ella Flynn told her about going around Brisbane to buy the suits of dead men. She had tuxedos of black wool flannel and gabardine business suits.

Roxy tugged the material from the haversack. It was still wrapped in the brown paper Leo's mother had mailed it in, her return address in the corner. She was not aware of Ella Flynn intentionally memorizing the address. It might have been simply that she had a very good memory. She had excelled in school because of that. She might have felt a little guilty. When Roxy commented on her shrine to the Virgin Mary, Ella Flynn felt a need to tell her that she had the highest average in religion in her eighth-grade class. Her memory made her a good seamstress, for she could go into a shop and try on a dress and eyeball the seams and darts and walk out knowing exactly how the dress was constructed. She would go home, make some notes to herself, and then she would sew up a dress exactly like the one in the shop. It was her gift.

She said, "She must like you quite a lot to send material."

"They're close," Roxy said, meaning Leo and his mother.

"So will ye marry the Yank?"

"I don't know about that."

Then Ella discreetly pulled back a curtain over a tier of shelves. She took out a box of tea. Roxy glanced away, but not before spying can after blue can of Bully Beef from Adelaide and stacks of Arnott's Sweet Biscuits. Her mouth watered at the thought of the sugar filling and the delicate wafers. Obviously, black market. So much the better, she thought at the time. Ella had the spirit to take care of her own, in any way she could. There was no man around, and from what Roxy had seen of the daughter, a pitted-faced redhead with rotting teeth and come-hither glances, there would not be any man around for long. They would come and go. She could see all that in a glance. Later, Roxy heard that the black-market goods were acquired by the daughter, whose waitressing job was a front for her presence at a bordello that served Yanks. She didn't want to get involved. She refused tea and said that she only wanted to pick out her pattern, be measured, and go. She was to meet Leo at the Y. She told Ella Flynn this.

She stripped out of her uniform so that Ella Flynn might measure her.

Tape measure in hand, Ella Flynn asked, "How old's your Yank?"

Mostly a good Catholic girl, Roxy told the truth. "He's twenty-two."

Later, she imagined that Ella Flynn brooded over this. Her own daughter was twenty-two. Why wasn't this Yank with the likes of her? She might have pictured her daughter marrying a Yank, moving to the States, the boy in a deaf school there, herself with a dressmaker's shop of her own. She wondered how she could transport the tailor's mannequin to the States. There had to be a way. She probably brooded and took out her dressmaker's notebook and wrote down what she'd memorized: Mrs. Marge Bosko, 310 South 3rd Street, Cumberland, Maryland. USA. "Not serious, are ye?" she had said to Roxy, who stood on a chair in her cotton slip. "A fellow so young."

"It's wartime, Mrs. Flynn. Who knows?"

"I would think not."

Later, Roxy considered her remarks, as she dressed for the show. She dabbed on the Coty lipstick his mother had sent, a color like eggplant, not her color, but she was grateful to have a new lipstick. She had sent presents to his mother. Books about Fiji and the Aborigines. A boomerang. Leo wanted to marry her, but she sensed that there would be trouble later on because of their age difference. She couldn't imagine it—being fifty when he would be forty-two. Fifty and past the change. Fifty and possibly arthritic, the way her own mother was. Or fat. But she could not imagine being fat. Lulu tells her that *fat* is not an acceptable word now. She will try not to use it again. She was compact, with legs that Leo said were great in shorts. And other fellows had said that she had beautiful eyes. Leo always said they were magnets. Magnets for him. That's what she thought about, getting ready for the show, his coaxing voice that had probably never said such things to a girl before. There was a special thrill because it was all new to him. Sometimes she thought, Why shouldn't I be happy? Why shouldn't we get married? When she tells Lulu this, Lulu says not to say girl.

The day the war in Europe ended Leo received word that he would ship out to Manila within twenty-four hours. He went to the chaplain he had trounced in poker and offered to return all the chaplain's money if he would marry them on the spot. This was against all rules. They were supposed to have waited six months, and permission was needed from their commanding officers. But the chaplain, a wizened man with smoke-stained teeth and a boozer's red nose, grabbed at the chance to get his money back. Leo Bosko and Roxy McAuliffe were married near dark, down on the beach, in a high wind. She wore the yellow dress. Leo placed a ring on her finger that he had purchased at a trash-and-treasure market. The ring fit his little finger; it nearly fit her ring finger. It would have to do. "Don't we have papers to sign?" she asked the chaplain. He would get the papers to them. What they had done was illegal, and severe military disciplinary action was threatened if you married without permission and the cooling off period. This deepened her casual willingness to break rules. What she felt for Leo occupied her beyond the rational ability to make clear-headed decisions. Most rules have seemed arbitrary to her ever since. Leo shoved a wad of Australian bills into the chaplain's hands. Their one witness, a nurse she'd befriended early on, skedaddled back to the barracks. A storm was brewing.

The bottom fell out of Roxy's world. They had spent fourteen months together. He was in Manila; she thought of going back to Sydney, to be near cousins. But the military did not see fit to accommodate her. Admiral Nimitz said that if the Emperor Hirohito's palace should be bombed, he hoped they would spare the Emperor's white horse. The admiral wanted a victory lap riding that white horse. The higher-ups had plans that did not include people like her.

"We're married," Leo said, in his letters from Manila. The letters were written in pencil. He had gone to Catholic school and had lovely handwriting. "In our hearts we're married." Once Japan surrendered, there were no more letters.

He did not know that she was carrying Lily, Norman's mother. Leo went home to Cumberland; he married someone else, spur-of-the-moment, possibly on a bender, when they'd gone to the tracks for a good time, a girl he'd known growing up on the south side, where his mother and father owned a corner grocery and lived upstairs. His mother died around the same time. Roxy knew all this because Leo's father—Mike Bosko—picked up their correspondence.

When she told him that she was pregnant, he was determined that she would be on that war bride ship. She couldn't bear to tell her parents. They had grown taciturn and sorrowful during the Depression. Her mother had repeatedly said that if she were to get in trouble she would disown her and never speak to her again. And she cleaved to that. She never visited Roxy in the United States; she never expressed interest in Lily. Some people have backbone laced with toxic stubbornness. Mike Bosko wasn't about to give up his firstborn grandchild just because Leo had gone off half-cocked, he said, and married someone else. He did not approve of the girl Leo had married; her family was Evangelical United Brethren and Republican. Mike was Catholic and a lifelong Democrat, a near Socialist, a union man, although he hadn't belonged to a union since he was young. Mike said that Leo's mother had gotten to Leo and convinced him Roxy wasn't right for him. An old maid. Their babies might be deformed in some way because she was so old. Ella Flynn had written to her about their age difference and that mattered to Marge Bosko.

The sea voyage was rough and seemed endless. Her roomie—a girl from Perth, engaged to a submarine repairman from Oregon—struck up a flirtation with a sailor and at night Roxy had to listen to them under the coarse manchester. Decorum flew out the window. Girls had dysentery. They traveled in a malodorous haze. She finally slept on deck, among the women who cradled their babies in their arms; she clung to a quart jar of drinking water.

She disembarked the war bride ship in Los Angeles and was immediately shuttled onto a passenger train to Washington, D. C., where she waited almost twenty-four hours in Union Station, that vast, gray terminal. Once or twice, she went out through the front doors to the fountain. How she wanted to sit on the edge of the fountain with her sore feet in the cool water. But she was keenly aware of being in a new country. She was confused, dehydrated, and longed for her mother.

Mother. She was to be a mother. A mother with no father for her child.

Mike Bosko met her train in Cumberland on a humid fall morning. He had a nest egg. That's what she thought at the time. She had never heard the words embezzlement or racketeering spoken out loud. She didn't connect those words to the Arnott's Sweet Biscuits in Ella Flynn's cupboard. She got to know Leo's father pretty well. He was single, a man who slapped on aftershave daily, a man who liked to play the ponies, a man who said the rosary a few times for the repose of his wife's soul, and then he got on with things. And what he got on with was marrying Roxy. It was a formality. For her resident alien card. It never occurred to her that he had a secret reason for putting the decrepit Tansy Hotel in her name and her name only. At that time most women did not own property. Most women could not secure loans from banks. The employment ads in the newspaper were divided strictly into *Help Wanted Men* and *Help Wanted Women*. In those early days she never had to apply for a job. She never had to file taxes. Mike Bosko took care of all that. As Lulu might say, her life was on the down low.

Whatever red tape had to be done away with, Mike would have a friend in a high place to take care of it. Once in a while, she would wonder about those marriage papers the chaplain in Townsville had promised that windy night. But he'd been reassigned to Manila. Leo was in Baltimore, with his new wife and his children, all born-again, baptized in a river. His father-in-law had set him up in a blacktop business that sounded surprisingly lucrative.

And Mike, although he passed away twenty years ago, has looked after her. He left money—cash money—hidden in the cellar of the Tansy in a fireproof box and money in the bank. And he never laid a hand on her. In return, she let him visit with Lily, take her to Mass on Sunday and to a horse farm for pony rides, and buy her fancy dresses that she often dragged through the mud or ripped on a fence. When she was seventeen, he gave her the money to backpack around Europe with friends. He paid her college tuition. In return, Roxy minded the store when he made frequent trips out of town on business. He'd send a car for her, a salt-rusted De Soto from before the war. She never questioned it. Now she knows he was part of a slot-machine ring. And beneath the slots were other murky sources of income. Young women were probably involved. Route 301 was the main artery before the interstate came in. Tourists, truckers, ne'er-do-wells, anyone passing through might have contributed to her upkeep. Mike had shortcomings; he wasn't troubled by using the women to his own ends. They never talked about it directly, only obliquely. Mike needed to confess, the way he might to a wife. Toward the end of his life, he would come late at night; she would go out and sit in the car with him, in the greenish light of the dashboard, sipping Jamaican rum from a pint bottle, and she would listen hard and gather all Mike's secrets to her heart.

At first Roxy had daydreamed that Leo might show up at the grocery when she was minding it for his father. Now she can't even remember the address of the grocery. Their eyes might have locked in a meaningful way. There wouldn't have been greasy teenage boys hunching over the pinball machines in the side room behind a beaded curtain. Leo might have desperately reached around and untied her white butcher's apron and tossed it aside. They might have turned the CLOSED sign to face the street and had sex in the back room, among the stock. The odor back there was vinegary and sweet. There were wooden mouse traps smeared with peanut butter in the corners. But Leo never came to Cumberland, so far as she knew. Mike went to Baltimore to play the ponies; he saw his other grandchildren then. And after that one older man, she lost interest in sex. It was too messy. Too fraught.

Lulu kneels on the floor, changing the baby's diaper. The baby tugs at her braids that hang straight down as if meant to be tugged. Her body and the baby's body are one. Roxy thinks of those women with dysentery on the war bride ship. The way, after a certain point in a woman's life, her days and nights are partly about cleaning up shit and semen and vomit and blood.

Like a swoon, a gentle dying, Roxy's nap comes begging. She pinches her upper arm to stay awake.

The Tansy was nearly falling down when Mike moved her into it. Whistle Pig is about sixteen miles from Cumberland and that seemed a long way in 1945. Now, it's not. People speed around the mountains at all hours of the day and night. And soon, she's told, there will be driverless cars. She doesn't trust that one iota.

Lulu grins sheepishly. She says, "It's not his."

Ah, a secret. An outsized secret. Currency. Currency she might spend.

"But you want it," Roxy says. How she tries to keep her voice neutral. If Lulu knew how much she depends on her and the children to keep her alive she might vamoose.

Lulu opens her iPad to swing dancers at the Denver airport. A flash mob, she calls it. She props up her iPad on the coffee table and snugs up close beside Roxy. She wraps her arms around her, making little bounce-dance moves, while Toots crawls back to the cooking pots. Roxy loves the girl in the video with long orange hair. She has faith in all the young people. Lulu does not hesitate to hug her, touch her. It's something they don't tell you about old age, cronehood, thornbackishness—people stop touching you.

"I want to be free. I don't want to be tethered to love."

Roxy thinks, That ship has sailed, honey. You've got babies. But she says, "My suite's empty. In the big house."

"Norman would kill me," Lulu whispers.

Norman could hold a grudge for life. Roxy herself no doubt has a short life, so let him. Lulu will be her very own. She whispers back, "He's never wanted for a woman long."

The old man sidles into view beyond the screen door. She hasn't admitted to Lulu that she knows who he is. At the Senior Center, he, too, departs when they start with the pool noodles. He's wearing a baby blue cardigan; his knuckles are gnarly on the walker handles; he keeps time with the swing dancers by tapping one foot.

His presence reminds her of the time she met Albert Einstein at the lake. Mike Bosko had taken her and Lily up there for a holiday. Lily was still a baby; Mike had asked the resort clerk if she were free to babysit after her shift. People did these things then, left their babies in the care of strangers in exchange for a few hours of freedom. They went to a party at a log cabin. It was early fall and chilly at that altitude. Mr. Einstein had asked her if she wanted to go for a walk and she said yes. Outside, they did not walk farther than a half-hidden stoop on the side of the cabin. Piles of dry leaves had pitched up there. Mr. Einstein said, "This seems inviting," and he made a little bow and thrust out one arm to encourage her to sit down. She hadn't thought of him in such a long time. It was 1947. People were beginning to feel optimistic about the war being over. It was a time in her life when she still wanted the attention of men.

Lulu hasn't burned herself out yet. She changes her earrings every day. She doesn't walk; she sashays. Despite breastfeeding Toots, another man, not her husband, has gotten his hooks into her, and she's pregnant. She has a low-key flirtatious manner, even with the man who sells lamb chops at the farmers market. At times like that Roxy fades into the background, almost as if they had agreed to it.

After flirting with Mr. Einstein, and the affair when she was almost forty with the man at the camera shop, Roxy had felt burned out. Back in that time women didn't always want to keep on. It was work, the fragile dresses, the girdles, the Toni home permanents, the nail polish, the nylon stockings and garter belts. Mr. Einstein had taken off his cardigan and draped it around her goose-pimpled shoulders. She had felt an erotic twinge because of his kindness. He was old; she had thought of herself as getting old.

"I thought you wanted to learn to play the banjo," Roxy says to Lulu. "I'll give you one for your birthday."

That's all it takes.

In this way they decide that Lulu will join the others, the women of Tansy. All the ramshackle spaces are supposed to be reserved for women artists, and right now Lulu is making babies. Over the years, the women of Tansy have had babies. But life is long. As Lulu might say, "It's early days." Some night when she's exhausted from nursing Baby #3 back to sleep, she might have an idea. A creative worm. Turning the compost of her disparate thoughts. Lulu, Lulu, Roxy silently petitions. The day I die I hope you're finding me a flash mob and pouring me a glass of red wine. What're friends for?

Apple & Palm

Maddy Keene thought it was sad—for her—and a little bit weird, that people would never laugh at a man who had lost his arm in a war or a child with cancer who'd had a limb amputated, but they thought nothing of laughing at people who did not have front teeth. The three months she'd gone to college—one eyelash of a lifetime—she had been friends with a girl who had a prosthetic leg, a hard-shell brown thigh and calf and foot, with clever joints that allowed each section to move so that the girl could wear a shoe and walk. She wore black-and-white Vans slip-ons, a checkerboard design. She got around with a bouncing, nearly cheerful gait. Her giggly voice and her boyfriend, a drummer in a band, seemed to imply that she lived the life of a standard eighteen-year-old. She'd return late to the dorm, her smug face chapped from kissing the drummer. Anyone getting close to sex seemed smug to Maddy. She didn't think she'd ever be kissed because of her fake teeth. With one wooden crutch, her friend would hop down to the dorm bathroom, in a textured white robe, a breezy absence where her right leg should've been. No one laughed at her. Maddy also knew a man—Wilder—with a disfigured face from some sort of accident. She knew Wilder as well as she could know anyone with Boone breathing down her neck all the time; Wilder sold grass-fed beef at the farmers market table next to the one she shared with Boone's mother. Wilder was a peaceful man, kind to everyone, revered by everyone. His brother, a clerk at the branch library, lived across the street from the farmers market at the corner of Apple and Palm. The brother wore a library name tag—Fox—and he always asked Maddy what she was reading. One hot day he invited Maddy and Wilder to leave someone else in charge of their tables and come over to his house for lemonade on his patio. Fox and Wilder were those kind of people—they made a habit of being generous. Wilder's pitted face and neck looked as if it had melted, as if heat had been applied. She could not imagine someone laughing at him because of his loss. Yet comics on TV and thoughtless men in taverns and teenage girls and educated people supposedly trained to not offend—teachers—snickered about people like Maddy who have lost their front teeth.

It happened when she was twelve and she was almost thirty-six the day her life ended.

She and her mother and two younger brothers had lived on a hilly gravel road in Maryland, four miles from the Delaware state line. Maddy's father did what her mother called his disappearing act. For months on end. She blamed her mother. Why couldn't she keep him at home? In a fallen-down shed near the disused chicken coop, she unearthed a treasure trove of True Confessions magazines that set down heaps of life lessons. She gathered that it was a woman's responsibility to keep a man. They drank well water that smelled like rotten eggs. Maddy had to hold her nose to drink it. If there was a drought month in summer, they ran out. They had it delivered by a man with a tank truck who sold a tank of well water for thirty dollars, cash Maddy's mother sometimes had to borrow from her mother, Gran Betty. A blackberry patch sprawled along the edge of a ravine where people abandoned appliances. And Maddy ever after had a sentimental longing for wild blackberries.

Every day Maddy's mother sprinkled used coffee grounds on the tile floors and swept up; she ironed to classic rock. Twice a summer she hauled her children and one friend each to Ocean City for the day, where they ate Thrasher's French fries, dripping with vinegar, and bologna sandwiches she had brought from home. A haughty neighbor woman, who never met your eyes, called how they lived "on the dole." Her kids teased Maddy about it. Food stamps. Little booklets of coupons like raffle tickets. Other people in the checkout line sneered or glanced away, embarrassed, whenever her mother sent her into Acme for groceries.

Maddy had a view of herself as huge, although when she met Boone, she seemed small, 116 pounds, slight of build. Easy to shove around. Earlier, she had to be big, a *big* girl, to be the big sister to her brothers. Maddy's first visit to the dentist was during one of her father's disappearances. The dole meant she could go to the dentist.

Maddy and her mother are pacing up and down the street outside the dentist's office in town. She's in a polka-dot shift and flip-flops. Her mother is agitated, her whirly black hair blowing in a hot summer wind. She's wearing jeans and flip-flops; she carries a tooled leather purse that contains her cigarettes, her keys, a Cover Girl lipstick, receipts, and little money. The dentist has prescribed pulling Maddy's front teeth. Her permanent teeth. Her only teeth. It is a moment that will change her life forever. She has cavities and he says there's nothing to be done. Later, Maddy gets it: There's nothing to be done that the dole will pay for.

Her mother leans against their car, a blue-and-white Ford station wagon from the seventies, its tires slick. Maddy's grandfather gave them the station wagon. He was always impatiently providing for them. Her mother jerks her purse open, plucks out a cigarette and lights it. A Kool. Her fingers are rough, but they have healed after the long winter of splits and cuts from firing the coal furnace around the clock. "There's nothing we can do," she says. "We have to do it."

When Maddy's period began a year later, her mother said, "Now you're stuck with it." The two events—getting her period and losing her teeth—were somehow plaited in memory.

Stuck with it. Stuck with being a woman and a girl with no front teeth.

They go back inside the brick dentist's office. Light from the kliegs bounces off the pharmacy-green equipment. Maddy is warned to be still—the dentist needs to concentrate. The needle in the roof of her mouth feels like a puncture all the way to her eyeballs. Her mother isn't beside her. Someone—a child, she thinks, as if she's not a child—cries almost hysterically, hiccupping, in the next examination room. She waits alone for the painkiller to take effect, for her mouth and nose and face to feel puffy. What she notices are her ragged toenails. She used to chew them, arms and legs wrapped like a pretzel, but she made herself stop at the start of grade six. The dentist speaks not a word. He wields pliers like a tool her father might have in his toolbox. His breath is warm on her cheek. His tuna breath. He extracts her four front teeth and each individual tooth coming out is a tug of war between her body and the dentist; she tastes the blood, surprisingly watery, salty. Finally, his assistant daubs at the holes in her gums with gauze. Blood, blood, everywhere, and she presses gauze into Maddy's mouth and tells her to clamp down.

And she does. Too stunned to weep, she clamps down. It feels as if she might choke on the gauze.

In exchange for this ordeal, she is allowed to spend the weekend in Rising Sun at Gran Betty's house, a rare treat. There is homemade peach ice cream, and a grapefruit cut in half, served with a serrated spoon, a nicety she has never seen before. Her mother's childhood now appears in focus as a luxury, something she hadn't understood when she was younger. Marrying Maddy's father has been a come down, a descent so rapid that they will never recover from it. This is why Gran Betty always says, "It's just as easy to marry a rich man as a poor man."

At her grandmother's, Maddy is allowed to do as she pleases, so long as she keeps to herself; reading is all Maddy ever wants to do. On her grandmother's shelf there are Readers Digest Condensed Books. She reads *The Winds of War* and *The Stepford Wives*.

That summer, she stayed close to home, reading novels about faraway places, baking blackberry pies, and trying not to look at herself in the mirror. She hated her face, her thighs, her linoleum brown hair. She divorced from herself by reading. No one—not the dentist or her mother—felt any urgency about providing her with what they called a bridge. She went around toothless for two months, feeling lumpish, fat. Right before the start of school she was taken back to the dentist's office and fitted with a plastic bridge. Every morning when she got up, a bridge was there to be inserted; every night when she went to bed, it was there to be cleaned, evidence of the life she lived as a girl, a life that entailed spreading shortening on her toast during times of scarcity, a life of sharing the gray bathwater. Until the day she died, every time she brushed her teeth, for a second, she was that awkward, somewhat pudgy, twelve-year-old girl, wearing coke-bottle glasses, standing on the hot sidewalk while her mother smoked a cigarette and decided her fate. With that wound she was awarded shame. "Play it safe," she commanded herself. Her father once asked, "Tight-lipped, ain'tcha, girl?"

To prove her worth, she went off to college on a partial scholarship as far from home as possible, but still in-state. She resisted the Gen Ed courses that seemed like high school. She had a passion for trips with the outdoor club, kayaking wild rivers, day hikes at Coopers Rock. Still, she could never imagine a straight line between those outings and getting a degree. For a few hours, outdoors, her shame dispersed in the mountain air. But shame has a way of tunneling into your heart of hearts. As hard to get rid of as fire ants.

She learned to pretend to smile spontaneously.

Then Boone came along. He drove truck for a beer distributor; Maddy met him on the sidewalk in front of Top Hat Liquors. After a rocky semester, she had gotten a job as a waitress at the cafe next to the liquor store. This all happened a long way from home and the person she had been when she lived at home. You wrote letters or called collect, which cost an arm and a leg, her mother said.

She was kissed. And then fucked, according to Boone. He taught her to say *fuck*. It was a shred of power she had over him, if she wanted it; Boone groaned with sex when she whispered fuck. *Fuck me.*

She got pregnant; they went to live in the trailer on the edge of a town called Whistle Pig. She tried to get blackberries started in the hardscrabble dirt behind the trailer she and Boone purchased for what he called a song—a freakin' song, Maddy. He said it as if he were putting one over on the seller, but Maddy suspected all along that it was no good deal; mice got in at a rotten place under the sink where there was black mold. That proved her right, but you never said I told you so to Boone. The berry canes failed to thrive.

It took Maddy a few years to learn about gardening. Along the way she had babies, all girls, Megan, Kelly, and Brianna, each one like her in her own way. She worried a little because the two older girls ignored Brianna, the baby. But Boone's mother—Ingrid—said they would outgrow it and love each other when they needed each other. After she got pregnant, Boone's kisses were few and far between. With gardening she had her specialties: soft-neck Italian garlic that braided neatly, asparagus, tomatoes. She cooked up batches of tomato chutney and sold it in jelly jars to tourists from Baltimore. After Maddy's grandparents died, her mother wrote to say that they were moving to Florida. She had her heart set on more sunshine. Even though you despise each other, Maddy thought. One brother joined the military and was killed in Afghanistan. Roddy, the younger brother, went for his real estate license and was too busy making money to write back to her. Maddy's letters petered out. They were not a close family—that's what she told Boone when he asked. She had the feeling that Boone tucked away that knowledge, a circumstance that allowed him free rein. No brother would be coming to visit for long. No brother would ever bring a shotgun to the house and carry Maddy and the girls away.

Still, she wanted the girls to know that they did have family. Sometimes, if Boone were away hunting, Maddy would get out a photo album and sit the girls down and explain the photos. Her grandmother Betty, in a lawn chair, holding her favorite chicken, its black feathers molting. Her mother and father when they were first married, before her father started disappearing. Her brothers, shirtless and barefoot, in front of a cornfield. Roddy holding a long-haired cat; she seemed to remember his little acts of cruelty to the cat, but she didn't tell the girls. She would say, Great-Grandmother Betty. She died of pneumonia. My mother and father—your Gran Keene. Grandpa Keene. "They live in Florida now." Uncle Roddy. Uncle Dale, he died in the war. And the girls would repeat the family names until they got older, got bored. Or confused.

Boone's mother Ingrid had berry canes to spare and told her where the best soil was for berries. Maddy liked to go out to the garden first thing in the morning, the hem of her nightgown dragging in the dew. It was her world, the green in delicate washes, the abrupt fecundity always begging for a little attention.

Ingrid lived down the road, on the other side of a copse of trees, her yellow porch light faint as a pinprick all night. Whenever Boone hit Maddy, she sought refuge with Ingrid, a mountain woman with a half-acre garden and a loom she worked to make rag rugs to sell. Boone's father was long gone. Boone manhandled his mother sometimes, when her first of the month check came. It was something she and Maddy had in common. That, and the Friday farmers market where they sold their wares under a faded royal blue umbrella they had found at the flea. When Maddy's girls were too young for school, they would go along to the farmers market. A little girl in braids perched in a too-big lawn chair attracted customers. Maddy and Ingrid had a rapport. They tenderly helped each other with all their chores.

Halfway through the market, Maddy would slip away to the public library. She chose her books hastily. At Ingrid's hatchback, she lifted up the lining where the spare tire was kept and she hid her books. The library card she slipped into Ingrid's glovebox. On market day, Boone would be at work when she brought the books into the trailer, and they went into a suitcase in the closet.

During thinning and picking, on Sundays, Boone allowed her, and later, Megan and Kelly, to work part-time at the orchard on the other side of Brick Mountain. Jill Zebrak, the old woman who owned the orchard, was a reader. She and Maddy would sometimes sit on her porch when the day was done, in wicker chairs, heads bent to the novels they were reading, while Megan and Kelly took turns riding the decrepit gray horse—a rescue named Buddy. When she was small, Brianna would play make-believe at their feet with little wooden dolls and a yellow plastic dump truck she carried around in a lunch pail. She would make the dolls sit in the bed of the truck and drive them across the porch planks to the very edge. Sometimes they fell over onto the top step, but they magically did not get hurt. Then Boone would charge invasively down the driveway to reclaim them, his tires rousing up dust clouds. Maddy would place a bookmark in whatever she was reading and slide the book onto the wicker table, as if it had nothing to do with her. The old woman—Jill—somehow understood.

When Brianna came in and found the bodies, flames leapt from behind the mica door of the cast-iron behemoth in the living room. Someone had built up the fire. Probably their father. Their mother—Maddy—would always hiss, "Put on a sweater," if they complained of being cold. They found her sticky notes—on the fridge, on the bathroom mirror—and the sticky notes read: Put. On. A. Sweater. She resented chopping wood. They lived partially off the grid. That's what their mother always said if they complained about the lagging dial-up internet. She said it like it was something to endure, and yet she was proud of it, too. Their father called the girls *gridders* or sometimes *gridder critters*. They never gave up wanting smart phones and constant hot water and Netflix.

The others were late getting home due to volleyball practice. Their mother lay on the bed, blood all around her like the velvet skirt around the base of a Christmas tree. Part of her face looked like meat in the meat case at Martin's. After that, Brianna couldn't be trusted to be sent to the back of Martin's to pick up a package of burger. Once she vomited at the meat case, and although the store manager was kind, he was also repelled—his whiskery face scrunched up—and he hastily ushered her out of the store.

Their father lay on the floor, his face half-hidden by the shadow of the bed, a bluish gun near his knee. It was a gun Brianna had seen before, in the glovebox of his truck. She didn't know what to think or feel until her sisters arrived home. Her whole body lurched into a gigantic shiver. She stuck herself into the back closet which was full of hidden books and clothes her mother had worn early in her life—a prom dress purchased from a Goodwill and a moth-eaten ski sweater. There was a cigar box of leftover Easter candy on a shelf. Addicted to candy, her mother always saved some back for herself. Brianna opened the box and roaches crawled out all over her hand. She flung them away and cursed out loud—*Jesus fuck*—something she never would have done in front of her parents. She didn't even know that phrase had lain dormant, waiting for her to use it. She crushed into the prom-dress and let the nylon net and beading scratch her arms and face. The dress smelled like a scent her mother had loved before she met their father: CK. A kind of sporty, independent smell. You could probably wear it playing volleyball, something Brianna wanted to do when she was old enough to spike it the way her sisters did, leaping higher than the net, pounding the ball with one fist. If you paid close attention, you could see the force of the spike all the way up her sisters' arms. She hoped they would teach her. She was tall like their father, a head taller than most of her classmates. She thought her sisters would pay attention to her when she turned ten. Double digits. They had taught her to ride a bike. She would wear CK and play volleyball.

Kelly was fourteen, and Megan was sixteen. Megan had changed her name to Finley, and wanted to be called Fin, but she hadn't told their parents. It was just a thing at the school bus stop. That's as far as she'd gotten. Brianna wanted to call her Fin, to see her smile, but it felt odd in her mouth and in her thoughts. Kelly had a girlfriend and thought she was lesbian. Brianna was the only one who had not deviated from what their parents expected, and now their parents were gone.

This was dumb, but she thought: Now I can get the job at the dog school. She had begged their parents to let her work at this old man's place down the road, close to the Potomac River and not far from the bike trail, but her parents had steadfastly refused. The old man called it dog school, but it was a one-man rescue facility. And the old man was a crusty grump. He lived alone. He collected compost from the neighbors for his garden and that's how Brianna found out that he wanted a girl to work for him. It was her chore to lug a bucket of compost down to his gate. He said that girls are more responsible than boys. Be that as it may, her mother had said, you're not working there.

You think you might like to do exactly what you want. But then your parents are dead, and it feels as if you have stepped off Dan's Rock into nothingness.

What kind of nothingness became clearer when her sisters came home. There was a quarter hour of screaming and crying. Tears running down their faces. Brianna's too. She went out to the front deck. Goldfinches—her mother's favorite—pecked at the sunflowers that were taller than the trailer. Brianna shrieked. She shrieked over and over, until Kelly came out and said, "Shut the fuck up."

Megan tried to compose herself and called the sheriff, hyperventilating as she told him. She called the old woman—Jill—at the orchard. The old woman said she would come right over and wait with them for the sheriff to arrive. Megan was having trouble catching her breath from the crying. Brianna sat on the edge of the sofa, shaking. She picked at the white threads of the knee of her torn jeans. Kelly pounded a pillow, her pimples turning to fiery red splotches on her cheeks. Megan didn't even have her license yet. How would they get anywhere to do anything?

When no one was looking, Brianna went back into the bedroom and took the book from her mother's hand. It was easy. She knew about rigor mortis from roadkill, but her mother's hand let go of the book as if Brianna only wanted to read a passage from it and would be giving it back. Without looking at the title, she stuffed it into her book bag. Kelly and Megan made mewling indecipherable noises in the living room, punctuated with curses or prayers. Brianna opened her mother's top dresser drawer and grabbed two bras, both faded and flowery. She had gotten in the habit of spying on her mother when she dressed. She was curious about bras and how you put them on. She had the notion that she would save them for the right time. That made her comprehend that—like a cartoon thought balloon—her life would be about more than this. Get me out of here, she pled. By that she meant, you get yourself out of this.

She went to the back porch and grabbed the white plastic compost bucket. It seemed only half full. The burning bushes her mother had planted long ago were red now. She dragged the bucket toward the old man's place. It was heavier than she thought it would be; she had to set it down and readjust the way she carried it. The metal carrying handle cut into her hand. I'm alive, she told herself. As she neared the old man's gate, a dozen dogs rushed up to the fence. Her favorite was a wiener dog who had deep brown eyes; he always seemed to be communicating directly with her. She hoped the old man would hear the uproar and come out. But Jill's truck came along, and the dogs focused on that, a frenzy of barking. Jill said, "Leave that and get in here." She did as she was told. Country music tinkled from the radio, trying to break through the static. Brianna became aware of a stinging scrape on her calf from the bucket's harsh edge. Her mother would have tended to her.

Jill wore warm weather clothes, even though the mornings were chilly now—long rough shorts with numerous pockets and a man's tattersall shirt, the sleeves rolled above her wrists. The flesh above her knees gathered in tiny brown pleats. She wore muck boots, the toes and heels spattered with dried mud. Her hair had not been brushed. She had pulled it into a knot at the back of her head, the loose gray ends spiraling.

Inside, right away, Jill sat down next to Megan and asked, "Fin, who can you go to?" She called her Fin.

She knows, Brianna thought. And she wondered, not for the first time, how do adults know what they know?

Megan gave Jill her full attention and said, "Nobody."

Jill said, "I'll say I'm your aunt."

Megan understood immediately. "They'll take us if you don't."

They knew about foster care. Their father had told them not to talk about family. He said, "Foster care might get you." Their mother explained it once and once was enough.

"They're not going to take you."

Kelly asked, "What about Gran Ingrid?"

"I've got the space. She'll see the wisdom in it."

Kelly said, "Shouldn't we ask?"

Brianna thought that she meant ask Dad.

"Won't she tell?" Megan said.

Brianna pictured Gran Ingrid's fallen-down house. She was a hoarder. You had to zig-zag through piles in each room to find your way. Her house reeked of cat. She fed a dozen or more and called them feral, but, soft-hearted, she allowed them to sleep inside in the winter. She was scorned by neighbors, but Brianna found the piles fascinating. Old sheet music and postcards with photos of dead people in their coffins. A collection of matched salt-and-pepper shakers that she was allowed to play with when she was small. Penguins. Foxes. Owls. And skulls with gold eyes. At Gran Ingrid's they made apple cider in a wooden press with a red wheel they cranked, the juice running down their arms. But the drinking glasses in her kitchen were always dusty, splotched with dried dish detergent. Brianna had to sleep with Gran Ingrid when she stayed there, and the sheets smelled bad. Jill—Aunt Jill—had a rescue horse and a dog. Her house was huge, with a sunporch. She baked these special cookies with oatmeal and nuts and chocolate chips. There was a shelter at the end of her driveway where, long ago, children must have waited in bad weather for the school bus. Maybe Aunt Jill would let her work before she was of age. Having her own money would open all sorts of doors.

But would Jill let her work at the farmers market with Gran Ingrid?

She had heard of pros and cons.

While Brianna added up the pros and cons of each, a decision was made. No one asked her what she thought.

She was used to it.

Aunt Jill—Briana took to the name. She had to. Aunt Jill was ancient—that's what their mother had said, with a peculiar kind of reverence. Her mother would never be ancient. She would always be frozen in time.

"I'll call her," Aunt Jill said. "It's better she hears it from a friend."

Megan grasped Aunt Jill's hand. Aunt Jill squeezed it once or twice but then she was all business. Brianna wished someone would hold her hand. Kelly was outside on the deck, smoking a cigarette she had filched already from their father's hidden carton. Out the picture window, the sky was lavender with sunset, a smidge of green at the horizon, like a chink you could possibly slip through, into another world. They would slip into another world.

Aunt Jill said they would sort it out legally later. *Legally.* Who did they belong to now? "After this—she might not be in any shape to take you."

That's how they ended up cramming clothes and shoes into plastic bags and moving to Jill's house. Aunt Jill's. Brianna felt an undercurrent of adventure and then a wash of guilt, as if ice water had been chucked over her head. Still, many times, in bed, in the dark, Megan and Kelly had whispered about running away. Was this what it felt like?

The sheriff seemed relieved.

Brianna saw how telling a lie might make everything easier. Also, not having to ask a man what to do, that came home to her.

The funeral—Gran Ingrid called it a memorial—was held three days later at the Legion. They had to get it over with, as soon as their Florida grandmother could get there. Their Florida grandfather stayed in Florida. Gran said that he wanted to take care of the dog himself, that the dog was his emotional support animal. He had a heart condition and had never flown in a plane. It was better this way. Brianna had heard the stories of his disappearing act, and this was another disappearing act. She thought it without judgement. She wished that she could disappear from the funeral. She hoped there would not be kissing. Kissing—what a profound embarrassment.

The Legion Hall was packed with people on the family side. Window air conditioners roared at each end of the room; people said it was Indian summer, but Megan whispered, "That's fucked. Not something you should say." Why was a mystery to Brianna. Gray folding chairs had been set up. Brianna wanted to be in the grown-up section of the Legion. It was dim, with a beery, greasy odor seeping out. Songs on the jukebox had been changed to reflect the moment: "Amazing Grace" and Elvis singing "How Great Thou Art." She had never been to a funeral and believed whatever anyone said and the way things were done seemed the way they should be done. Gran Keene from Florida sat in the front row and cried into crumpled tissues. She made a pile of the tissues on the floor. Megan brought her a wire trash basket and set it beside her chair.

Uncle Roddy came. And women she thought she recognized from old photos. Her mother's aunts. Brianna reminded herself: Uncle Dale died in the war. Other family lived far away, and Brianna took distance to heart. It seemed impossible to her that people moved around the country and around the world. She knew nothing about money and how it worked and what might be possible with money. Roddy had said that he was sure that their mother wanted to be cremated.

"Get your story straight" was something her father had said to her. The story she had to get straight was that her father had murdered her mother. Ashamed, his mother—Gran Ingrid—went along with whatever Roddy said. Nobody wanted to sit near her in the Legion Hall. She sat off to one side on a bench near the door. Brianna went up to her and hugged her. Her clothes smelled like garden work: sunlight on marigolds and dust.

She asked, "You'll come to the market with me, won't you?"

Brianna thought: Apple and Palm. She imagined going to the house where Fox the librarian lived. He would give her books. A country girl, before she had read the green street signs at the corner near the farmers market, she didn't know anything about town life. She had always pictured an apple in the palm of a hand until her mother said, "Palm trees. I'd like to see a palm tree someday."

Aunt Jill came and sat beside Gran Ingrid.

There were no caskets, no bodies. On a folding table, there were two velvet bags, like gift bags, that held their ashes. Brianna wanted to see the ashes, but she was afraid to ask. Roddy said, "We'll scatter the ashes at the lake." Roddy lived at the lake now, Brianna knew that much. He sold vacation houses to people from the city.

Someone had set up a framed enlarged photocopy of Boone and Maddy's wedding photo. Boone was wearing a tropical shirt. Maddy, a peasant dress. Boone had his arm around her, his fingers pressing against her left breast. A black scarf had been draped across the top of the frame. It was a seasonal scarf, with tiny indistinct pumpkins embroidered on it, all they could find at the last minute.

Most of the faces were a blur at first. Not too many relatives. Mostly neighbors and teachers. Before Gran Keene moved to Florida, even though the drive took forever, all the way to the other edge of the state, they had gone to her house for Easter dinner. There had been a big ham with cloves all over it. And Easter candy in bowls. Brianna was allowed to help herself. She had hidden under a bridal veil shrub when the goodbye kisses began. She was coming out of a childish fog where she didn't grasp familial relationships. She knew mother, father, sisters, grandmothers, but in what she already called "normal life" she hardly saw everyone else.

"They're just curious," Megan said, curling her lip, snarling, sending mean daggers out her eyes to all the people filing in, their heads hung down apologetically. She couldn't even spot Kelly, who had decided to wear a camouflage shirt over her black T-shirt and skort. Kelly had a way of edging outdoors whenever she didn't want to put on manners. No adult was in charge of them anymore.

Women were depositing bowls and disposable aluminum baking pans of food on a long table. Brianna spied cupcakes.

She had been marched to the front by Megan and made to sit down at the end of a row. If only she could melt into the center of the row, to avoid people. She could think about the gray horse, how he had pulled back his pink lips and taken a carrot from her flat palm. Megan said, "Stay here. I'll corral Kelly." If Megan were shooting daggers, she—Brianna—would be sweet as sugar pie. A man sidled through a knot of people and halted beside her. She craned her neck and stared straight up at him; he was Fox, the librarian, the brother of the man who had the melted face at the farmers market. She had gone to his house with her mother and sat outside and sipped sour lemonade from pint jars. Apple and Palm were the cross streets. His house was painted two colors: yellow and pale green. Things matched. Yellow flowerpots. A green wreath on the door. A green bench. Her mother had gone inside for what seemed like a long time and when she came out, she had an armful of books he had lent her. They hid them in Gran Ingrid's car.

He works at the library, her mother had said. She had also said: "Don't tell Dad." This came back to her, doing her best not to fidget. Fox squatted down beside her chair and whispered, "Do you remember me?"

She nodded her head vigorously, trying not to smile because smiling was surely wrong at this moment.

He handed her a paperback book. *Woman on the Edge of Time*. "This was next. She wanted to read this next." He said, "When you're older, you might like it."

October, and it was hot despite the air conditioners. The weather was out of whack. A preacher up front, the underarms of his black suit dark with sweat, had the annoying habit of saying, "Don't-cha know." He swam before her eyes. His voice wavered in and out. "Don't-cha know that these two loving parents would have wanted the souls of their babies to be saved. By the Lord Jesus Christ." Oh, that was wrong. The word loving made tears pop into Brianna's eyes, but she held them back.

When the preacher finished, everyone was touching everyone else. Shaking hands. Patting each other. Uncle Roddy came over and scooped her up and carried her—she was too big to be carried—into the grown-up section of the Legion. Different music played hushedly behind the bar: some love song. She went along innocently, pretending to be innocent. He sat her up on a bar stool. Her dress crept up and her bare legs stuck to the red vinyl, which was ripped, and the duct tape patch hurt the backs of her thighs.

"You'd like a coke, I betcha," Uncle Roddy said. He stood behind her, his big hands rubbing her shoulders. Something clotted in his voice. She hoped he wouldn't hug her.

This brought to mind a time when he dunked her at the lake, before she knew how to swim. He had organized what he called a family reunion at a cabin a friend had lent him for a weekend. Their father didn't go. He said he had no time for frivolous trips to the lake. Later, Gran Keene would show up, possibly with children. Second-cousins! Brianna was trying to understand how everyone was related. Uncle

Roddy had lined up a few liquor bottles on a sideboard next to a stack of board games. The liquor bottles glimmered in the sunlight slanting into the dining room. They'd have some fun, he said. "That's not my idea of fun anymore," her mother had said.

Late afternoon, and wind riffled the lake water. She had goosebumps. Kelly and Megan had swum out to a floating dock. They were sunbathing out there, pretending to be older.

Her mother had gone back inside to change clothes. Uncle Roddy's girlfriend went along with her, rhinestone sandals dangling in one hand.

Brianna's swimsuit was too small, a hand-me-down. Her bottom showed. She knew that. Uncle Roddy swept her up onto his shoulders and held her ankles. Once he let go of her ankles and reached around and squeezed her bottom. It felt like a tickle between her legs. Out in the murky water, he slouched over and let her fall in. She came up shocked, crying, coughing hard, her lungs stinging. He pretended to rescue her, carrying her gently in his arms. Later, on a striped bedsheet they used as a beach blanket, he offered her a sip of beer from a can. It burnt her mouth. She knew it was wrong. She knew he had crossed a line. She crossed it with him, even though she was only six years old.

That was three years ago. She knew so much more now.

If her mother had been at the Legion she would have restrained Brianna by grasping her upper arm until it hurt. Or giving her a little, almost unobservable, shove between her shoulder blades. It was her way of protecting her. She didn't want her to talk to strangers or be touched by strangers. Uncle Roddy was not a stranger. That's why she always hid when it was time for goodbye kisses. It was coming back to her now. If she didn't hide under the bridal veil or in the shed, he would put his big warm hands on her cheeks and flick her lips just once with his tongue—not so anyone would notice.

That night she started reading *Woman on the Edge of Time*. The pages were brittle and yellow as pee. On one of the blank back pages of the book, someone had written, in blue ballpoint: "I can't stop thinking about you." She leaned over her daybed and tugged her book bag out from under it. The book she'd taken from her mother's hand was titled *The L-Shaped Room*. On a blank page in the back of the book there was her mother's handwriting: "I'm trying hard not to think it."

A bleeding woman was on page one. There were words she was shocked by, thrilled by—whoring, cunt—and words she did not know, like *grifo*. The blood was too much. She tossed the book under the daybed. She closed her eyes against the light of the ceiling fan.

Aunt Jill had given her a choice about where to sleep. She could have the daybed in the sunporch, or she could have a storage room upstairs that contained a few boxes, some canned goods, a camp cot, and suitcases. She chose the sunporch.

Aunt Jill came in, flicked off the light, lifted the bottom of the comforter, and laid in a hot water bottle against her feet.

"It gets chilly out here."

Tears sprang into her eyes; she pinched her eyes shut to force them back. The tears clumped in her throat. The hot water bottle caused the tears. The kindness. For the first time, but not the last, she thought: I will never see my mother again. Never. That *never* was like a hammer in her mind. Everything up until the hot water bottle—finding them, packing up, the funeral, sitting with Uncle Roddy in the grownup side of the Legion Hall while he drank a whiskey that swirled like caramel, his hand on her knee—all of it was a puzzle, a test you had to take. The test had kept her busy. Until she felt the warmth of the hot water bottle. She still had her socks on. Aunt Jill squeezed one of her feet. With gruff affection.

"Where's Kelly? Where's Megan?" Her voice felt croaky, whispery.

"They're out at Harper's." Harper had been introduced to them at the start. She was Aunt Jill's true niece. She had something wrong with her foot. Why wasn't she invited out to Harper's place? It was an old shed named Early Bird, and Harper herself was old, at least thirty. At night there were solar lights along a fence line that led to Early Bird and Early Bird itself was all lit up with tiny white lights strung along the deck. She saw the divide. Harper, Kelly, and Megan would be like sisters. She would be an orphan. Self-pity lumped in her throat.

"They wanted a sleepover."

"What about Gran Ingrid?"

"Her heart's broken."

Abrupt car headlights bounced down the rough driveway. Aunt Jill said, "Be right back."

It was Uncle Roddy. Uncle Roddy talking too loud to himself. Uncle Roddy stomping hard on the front porch. Uncle Roddy knocking hard on the front door.

Brianna shuddered, her heart vibrating, and she decided to pretend she was asleep. But she could hear them. Not every single word. But what Roddy wanted came across and Aunt Jill's response. Their voices were raised to travel through the glass of the front door. The dog named Braeburn growled menacingly.

"I need to see 'em."

"They're sleeping."

"They need family."

"You go home now, Roddy. We can discuss it when you haven't been drinking."

"Open the door."

"I'm not going to do that."

Then a car door slammed. And the headlights reversed their course back to the main road.

Her mother had never said no to Uncle Roddy. Brianna guessed that she wanted to feel close to someone who knew her before. Before Brianna existed. Or Megan or Kelly. Or before she met their father in front of Top Hat Liquors. She told them that story more than once. It occurred to Brianna that her mother believed in love. She wondered, Should I? As if belief in anything were a choice, a destiny you made up yourself, a future, instead of a cloud above your existence, either bright with sunshine or moody, stormy.

She must have drifted off.

Aunt Jill's hand was on her forehead.

A barn light shined right outside. Wind blew down a sheaf of red leaves. Old glass rattled in the panes. Was something skittering under the bed? She was afraid of bats. Bats could shimmy into tight little slits under doors or where the roof met the wall. The big dog named Braeburn nosed into the sunporch. He came directly to the daybed and eased himself up on to it. Something changed at that moment. She'd been chosen, infused with body-joy. She put her arm over Braeburn's back and Braeburn—who smelled like grass—lay his head on the edge of Brianna's pillow.

"What did he want?"

"What would he do with three girls to take care of?"

"We'd have to switch schools."

"Nobody's switching schools. But you might want to stay home for a few days."

Outside, the barn light winked on tin pie plates that were there in the strawberry bed to scare away birds. The light made her think of her mother after a fight. She would take a lantern and, in the dark, make her way to Gran Ingrid's house. He would drive away in the truck. Brianna would watch her mother's lantern bob in and out of the woods. Like the pie tins holding the light now.

Aunt Jill said, "I'm going to teach you to drive the farm truck."

"Me?"

"You'll need a couple cushions under you. You're tall enough. On the weekends there's plenty needs to be done."

Brianna pictured herself in the driver's seat with the window down. When her sisters staggered out of Early Bird, she'd shout, "Fin! Kelly! I'm driving!" And Fin might shout, "That's awesome, Bree!" She might.

What Goes Around

Jill Zebrak was parked in the shadowy casino parking lot. Delicate strings of Christmas lights in holiday shapes—a tree, a wrapped gift, a Santa—were visible in the distance across the dark lake. You could pay a fee and tune your radio to a certain station and the light show synchronized with Christmas tunes. Jill had never done it—she's too frugal for that, too cheap, some might say—but if you live near the state park and the casino, you can't help but know about it. Winter wind buffeted the car. She was bundled in a parka made for the far north, but she lived in the mountains of Western Maryland.

Papa was inside. She had always called him Papa, and eventually everyone in Whistle Pig would, too. She refused to go in. Since she had taken away his keys to the pickup, once a week she dropped him at the casino and went to the library until it closed. Old grudges and resentments die hard, and Jill blamed gambling for the troubles of her childhood. Papa lived on her property in a building outsiders might have called a shed. His choice. Although she won't pretend she wasn't relieved when he said he wanted an outbuilding, that somewhat insulated shop with a wood stove and a nearby privy, rather than a room in her house. Grown accustomed to being alone, she felt he might be under foot. All those things that happened long ago were squirreled away, and in the day-to-day she was able to compartmentalize. She looked after him, minimally, realistically, not benevolently—that is, she wasn't sentimental. Not about him. He was eighty-three. She was sixty-four.

She wasted gas and turned on the heater—just for ten minutes she told herself—and she read by the feeble glow of a light that clipped to her book, a novel about a girl growing up in Norway in the 14th century. She loved the way the characters took off on their rudimentary skis for a distant place and slept under animal skins.

Her phone lit up with a text from Harper, her grandniece in Pittsburgh. Harper sent a photo of herself with Doug, her sweetie, outdoors somewhere; it was frosty looking, a holly tree in the background, and she held up her left hand to show off an engagement ring. There was no message except a hashtag: #springwedding.

That was probably the only news that could make her go into the casino. Good news.

Wind gusts knocked her off balance, and she grabbed at car door handles to steady herself. The casino emitted a welcoming artificial fore-dawn light; a greeter stood at the ready to open the door. He wore earmuffs and a parka like hers. The temp was in the high twenties.

Inside was a coffee shop, with muted televisions tuned to football games. A wide hallway opened into the casino proper, its garish 24/7 eyeball-popping diversions going full tilt. A cavernous space, like the big box stores she tried to avoid. She went at finding him systematically, up and down the blocks of game machines—Sultan's Palace, Cherry Bombs, Easy Money—out to the noxious smoking balcony, and finally around to the bar, where he was lodged in front of a poker machine, a beer half-finished in a curvy glass beside the machine, and a young bartender with a metal ring in her eyebrow idly chatting with him while she dried a glass. She looked somehow familiar. Jill could see in his sly alert stance that he hoped the bartender was flirting. He would never give up the notion that he was a magnet, a charmer, for all women, old or young, gorgeous or homely—they were all worth flirting with and he never grasped how they indulged him, smirking ever so slightly, rolling their eyes. A geezer many times over.

The bartender saw Jill bearing down on him. "Looks like you're busted."

Papa turned, grinning.

A woman emerged from a nearby restroom and sat down intimately next to him. She put her hand on his thigh. It lingered there. Adele Pratt. A potter. Jill knew her from way back. They had gone to school together when Jill moved back to Whistle Pig on her own, a junior in high school. When she thinks, "We went to high school together," she doesn't mean they were friends. Adele ran with the greasers, the rough crowd. She had to overcome being named Adele. Now the name was in fashion, but then it was stuffy, reminiscent of the early 20th century. Jill might have wanted to run with the rough crowd—they were known for Friday Night Specials, a place by the creek at the edge of Adele's grandfather's farm where that crowd, Adele's, drove or walked to every Friday night, along a shoddy road, all ruts and mud most of the time, and around a bonfire they partied, and sometimes spent the night in sleeping bags and smoky blankets, and woke up in emotional ruin—but Jill had clung to her role as an outsider, a perch of safety. Adele was around Jill's age, with a puckered smoker's mouth, dressed in loose woolen clothes, with silver hair she probably hadn't cut in decades. Jill had run into her other places. In her younger days, Adele had taken over or tried to take over whatever space she occupied. Strutting around in a boyfriend's leather jacket. Riding without a helmet on the backs of motorcycles. She still wore those fuck-me boots with heels that announced her presence when she strode into a bar or cafe. But Jill knew for a fact that she was waiting for someone—her granddaughter Reenie?—to pick her up and trundle her home to the Tansy—an artists' co-op—where she lived with five other women, all of them related somehow. Adele had also been persuaded to give up driving at night. In a town the size of Whistle Pig, word gets around. Though they were the same age, Jill felt a mental harrumph of superiority because she wasn't anywhere near to giving up driving after dark.

They nodded to each other.

Now she understood why her father spruced up for trips to the casino. He had showered and shaved. Smooth as a baby's butt, he liked to say, rubbing his chin. He dabbed on Pinaud Clubman, a drugstore aftershave he always used. He clipped his nails.

With a little head jerk in Jill's direction, as if she'd be easily cowed, he patted a stool, while Adele leaned into the bar. He rubbed his index finger over dollar bills stacked on the bar like new linen napkins.

"Harper's getting married," Jill said.

"You don't say."

"Your enthusiasm is contagious."

"Harper's the only girl in the family," he said to the bartender and Adele.

"Except for me," Jill said.

"Wow," the bartender said, dispiritedly. "That must be rough."

Adele Pratt snorted.

"Let's go home."

"Aw, Jilly," he coaxed. "Let me finish."

As if there were ever an end to gambling.

Jill said, "Papa, I'm going. This's important. I want to get home where it's warm and quiet and talk to Harper. You, too. You need to congratulate her." Harper felt removed from the family history that cast her great-grandfather as a villain. She knew the sketchy details, but rage and blame had been extracted from the story of Sissy dying. Harper liked to play cards with the old man; she liked to bring him a fifth of whiskey and tip a glass in cheer, out in the shop with the wood stove roaring.

"I'll bring him back," Adele said, squirming in her seat.

Jill did not want to ask about the driving. She must have had a dubious look on her face because Adele said, "Reenie, she's coming to get me. She won't mind."

"Papa?"

Papa was intent on his poker machine. "Sounds good to me," he said.

Adele rubbed a proprietorial hand on his back. "We won't be long." Her hand was dry and whitish with clay. A working woman's hands.

Now was not the time to remind Papa that Iris—his ex and Jill's mother—had told Harper that if she ever got married—hitched, Iris called it—she would take the train from Montana to Pittsburgh for the wedding. Even though her mother was what Jill called an over-the-back-fence feminist, and Iris often said that marriage closes off your options, and "love's slavery" is part of her running commentary on sex and relationships, she had said she wanted to see Harper, her only great-granddaughter, go through this rite of passage. It was years ago when Harper was a slip of a girl. But it seemed like something you don't just say and then renege on. Papa hadn't seen Iris in forever. Since he got out of jail. Since the sorrowful time that stretched into years after Sissy died in a car accident when she was four. Jill's mind, and no doubt Harper's mind, leapt to these eventualities: a train ticket, fetching Iris from the station, making sure she was comfortable in a little bed and breakfast up the road from the orchard because Jill could not see Iris agreeing to stay on the same property as Papa, who was, as she saw it, responsible for the death of one of their children. Women predict the details. A wedding in the orchard like they had always talked about, blossom season, a reunion of everyone in the family still alive.

Jill Zebrak's family split up in the 1960s. Some of them lived in Maryland, some lived in Pittsburgh, some of them stayed in Montana. Far flung, she thought, but not as far flung as some families she had heard of. A woman with a short, man's haircut who stopped at Jill's farmers market stand had children living in Honduras and Portugal. The woman made it sound like something to brag about, but it must have been a lonely life, seeing her children on the flat screen, not being able to reach out and hug them, if you were a hugger. Some were not, or they were, but they managed to raise children who did not want to be touched. The 1960s was a time when ordinary people did not move around like they do now; they might have been considered unusual. When Jill left Montana when she was sixteen and on her own, she had little to her name, but she wanted to be back in Whistle Pig where she'd been born, where the rivers did not freeze over hard in winter. There was a secret history to her family's life in Whistle Pig; that secret history was like a defect in her house that she couldn't see, something to do with wiring or plumbing, say. Something that might require attention at some point.

Iris had decided not to come back.

Jill's early childhood had been spent in view of the Allegany Front, like a smoky blue woman taking a nap in the distance. But when she was eight years old, Papa took it into his head to move to Montana where his Aunt Mina lived. Iris's parents had passed away young from heart attacks; Papa's parents had faded into public housing in Baltimore; he seldom saw them. He told Iris she had no reason to stay in Whistle Pig. She was an only child. Once she told Jill that's why she wanted so many babies. They drove to Montana when summer makes every road trip fine. A lark, crossing all those states. Iris was pregnant with the twins, Sissy and Dan. They camped wherever they could; they bought food in grocery stores and ate their meals in parks. Papa got a job on a logging crew. They rented a little house in a small town, almost a village, not far from Bozeman, and they hunkered down during the winter and stuffed crumpled sheets of newspaper inside the walls. They learned to bank the wood stove at night to keep embers alive; they learned to take a little hatchet and shave curls of pine to use for kindling. Iris sometimes said, "You can't eat the goddamned scenery."

Did Iris ever have a happy moment there? Yet she's the one who stayed. And Dan. And Aunt Mina.

Jill felt a certainty about being where she belonged: Whistle Pig. In the middle of an apple orchard. And how many people can have that kind of certainty? It was like a stash of money in a coffee can or a full pantry. The carved sign at the end of her driveway read: Happy Trails. Apples. Jill Zebrak, Prop. To find her, you drove past the medical clinic until without warning the blacktop narrowed and wound up Brick Mountain in tight curves. There were no yellow lines; there were no guardrails. She was surrounded by wildlife areas, the boundaries of which the bears didn't mind. At least once a year she called the DNR, and they came out and lured the offending bear into a trap with sardines. They used aversive therapy—pepper spray and firecrackers and rubber pellets on his rump when they let him go. The sign out front was made of walnut, and Jill was solely responsible for maintaining its finish with tung oil. She was solely responsible for everything that it's humanly possible to be responsible for. Weather—rain and drought and cold and heat—was her contrary comrade; weather had an almost animal feel, akin to the bear and deer and possums. Her brother Leo, Harper's grandfather, lived in Pittsburgh;

every time they met, he asked her why she lived so removed from what he called *the rest of life*. Or sometimes he said, "There's more to life than feeding yourself." Jill usually said, "It gives me a kick just to see my name stamped on those wooden bins. In pruning season, I don't love the wind the way it cuts into me, but I know I'm alive. And the blossoms in spring—come then and we'll see what you think."

There was no season she didn't love. She told him about bringing a Coleman jug of fresh iced tea to the people who worked for her and how they translated the lyrics of their music and shared a laugh over the immutability of heartache in any language. "El Ultimo Beso." Mockingly, she said, "The last kiss." *If I'd known this would be our last kiss, I'd still be kissing you.* Teasing, like kids. That longwinded answer gave Leo pause. Sometimes Jill ended a day realizing she hadn't spoken to anyone except her dog Braeburn. When Leo visited, she talked his ear off.

She was meant to live in an orchard of her own, but she took a circuitous route getting there. And for a long time, she shed the stuff of memories as she went, thinking, as young people do, that anything painful was best left behind or hidden. Souvenirs of dead-end streets or trauma.

Papa did not come back by ten, as agreed. Jill texted Harper and said that they would call soon. Meanwhile, "Congratulations to you both!" That's what you say now, isn't it? Time was, only the groom was congratulated upon engagement, like the prince who wins the hand of his intended. His prize. His lofty goal. Iris would say, to have a woman to take care of him. But it didn't work that way now, so she congratulated them both and promised to telephone when Papa was available. That's how she put it. She took her arthritis medication that kept her from waking in the night with the icepick pain. Sleep was like that dark and silent gate Bonnie Raitt sings about.

The next morning, she set a kettle on the gas eye to boil and stood trying to decide whether to take her coffee back to bed or not. She listened to sleet patter into the gutters and then on into the cistern. A well would have been a good idea years ago, but they were on a mountain and the soil her trees were planted in was only so deep and after that it was rock. Various neighbors at houses nearby had tried to dig wells and they never succeeded. They often spent a small fortune—enough to send the well-diggers' children to college several times over—and there was never water. They had to haul water or, more likely, have it hauled. Most of them were younger retired people who had moved to the mountains from one city or another—DC or Baltimore or Philadelphia—and they got the land cheap, built their houses, and had to have water hauled, every single drop they used. But Jill made do with the cistern. She was used to the sound the rain and sleet made filling it up. She let Braeburn out to pee and then the dog barked his low-key *let me in now* bark and when Jill flicked on the porch light and opened the door, she saw clumsy Adele Pratt picking her way in those boots, headed from the shop to the back door. Adele's hair was ratty and flat. Jill thought how much messing she must have to do with it to be dolled up as she had been at the casino.

"My phone died," Adele said. "I need to call for a ride. Could I use your landline? Ham said I might could."

"Be my guest," Jill said, as if it were a perfectly normal event for Adele to have spent the night with her father. He was old enough to be Adele's father, but at their ages, what difference did it make? Some people might say no difference. But it irked Jill.

While Adele telephoned, Jill took her coffee across the way, into the living room, even though the kitchen and living room were all one big space. She turned on a lamp and pulled an afghan over her lap and picked up the book about the

Norwegian girl, as if to read. Braeburn took sides and lay down snugged up to the chair where Jill sat. She pretended to read.

Adele hung up and said, "This's a nice place." And, "Thanks for letting me use the landline."

Without looking up, Jill said, "No problem."

"Sure is quiet out here," Adele said. She shivered. "I was a little nervous walking in the dark."

So she was the kind of person who did not understand the social cue of a person picking up a book and sticking her nose in it.

"I'm reading," Jill said.

It was about one hundred yards from Papa's place to the house. Harper had strung white solar-powered lights—she called them fairy lights—on the fence along the way. Still, it was mostly dark. Jill had no patience with people who could not walk in the dark. If Adele was in the habit of not going home at night, she might have stashed a flashlight in her big ugly fringed bag. She might have a toothbrush in there. A tube of lube. And a phone charger. But she had not been prepared. She had probably gone into the casino planning to spend ten dollars on the slots and then call it a night.

Leo telephoned right after Adele went out to wait for her ride. Leo, who did some kind of business job. White-collar. He felt pride, she knew for sure, that he did not do manual labor like logging, as Papa had. He went to college and studied something to do with numbers, something he never tried to explain to Jill, and she wouldn't have wanted to know anyway. It bored her to even idly wonder about it.

"This's bad news," Leo said, "but not as bad as it could be."

"What're you saying?"

"Harper's been in a car accident." A garbled choking sound came over the phone, Leo squeezing tears back.

"Is she all right?"

"She's not all right. But she's alive."

A hot lump of anxiety spread the width of Jill's chest. Her hand shook holding the receiver of the landline, still warm from Adele's hand, and that felt sickening.

"Should we come up there?"

"We?" Leo asked, incredulously. "Don't bring him."

"How's Ryan doing?" Ryan was Harper's father, a firefighter.

"Holding it together," Leo said. "They were waiting for you to call. At Doug's place, you know, so they could both talk to you. To *both* of you." He went right up to the brink of accusation. She felt it, oh, yes. It felt like a slap. "She decided to drive home. She needed to get up early for work today. The bridges were icy. Black ice. She spun out and hit another car." There was a long pause. "No one died."

Not like that other accident when they were kids. Not like that. No one died. No one drowned. No one's body was lodged under ice in a river until spring thaw. Jill felt a singular mutual memory, a violation, take hold of herself and Leo. And the blaming. She wanted to blame someone. She settled on Papa. In the shadows, Adele Pratt was the auxiliary recipient of blame. Adele Pratt, with her coral lipstick, her dangly earrings, the furtive way she put her hand on Papa's thigh when they roosted in front of the poker machines. Two old people trying to stir up the ghost of chemistry.

In 1963 Jill was in grade six at a brick schoolhouse in that town—a hamlet—outside of Bozeman, Montana. So far away. Almost as if another person experienced it. She lived in swatches of memory, yet she pursued connections. It had come to her late in life to investigate family history.

She wanted to give Harper a book, a journal, of family stories going as far back as possible. She was Jill's only beneficiary, and the family member most likely to, if not treasure, at least appreciate their history. Unique among the young people Jill knew, Harper wanted to have children of her own. She hadn't given up on the planet.

Genealogy is a hobby many people have taken up. It makes money for someone—the genealogy corporations, right? Late in the evening, awash in the blueish glow of her laptop, her hips aching from sitting so long, bourbon and ginger beer beside her forgotten in a glass of melted ice, she came up for air and wondered, what are we getting out of this? The romance of ancestors who were cheese makers or innkeepers in Europe was making a silk purse from a sow's ear, as Iris would say. In her mid-eighties, Iris's speech ran to folkish sayings that she learned from *her* mother. And now Jill did that, too. She was old or on the verge of being old.

Here's something she remembered all on her own, without walking out to question Papa in his shop on a wind-scoured ridge near the bee boxes, without emailing Leo, without calling up Iris and pestering her to delve where she might not want to go.

It was the custom on Thursdays to bully anyone wearing purple—the sign of a queer. Queer was the only word they used. They did not know fag or gay or dyke or butch or trannie. Or ace. That was the new word. Ace. More importantly, Jill hadn't a clue what being queer meant. That is, beyond French-kissing, the nitty-gritty of the sex act, any sex act, was like a photograph yet to develop in a darkroom tray. They were sheltered in a way that children today are not. They saw the rough side—out-of-work drunks lurching from the Slabtown Tavern, a man shoving his wife, a fistfight, a man taking off his belt to threaten a child—but details of sex were hush-hush. You had to find it out on your own. She knew that there was something—troublesome—that her mother and her friend Madge were keeping from her. It was something they found hilarious, as well as heartfelt and burdensome. They would sit at the round oak table, sipping Mogen David wine from carnival glasses, nudging each other into oblique confessions.

In her stocking feet, near the wood stove, Jill would pretend to read a library book, so silent that they must have known she was storing up every veiled phrase.

And this:

The Pope was dying. It was on the radio every half hour.

They weren't Catholic, but in Montana Iris was taking catechism lessons from Father Brennan who came to their house twice a month. She had the notion that converting might keep her wayward husband at home. He had been raised Catholic by his old-country family, Bohemian women who had come as children to the New World, in steerage, in 1907. They had landed in Baltimore, moved to Whistle Pig, and eventually the last one still living—Aunt Mina—followed her daughter, an itinerant musician, to Montana. Aunt Mina had been close to Papa. Now it's conventional wisdom that you can't change men. But then, women felt it was their duty to change them, civilize them. Iris's eyes shone with hope whenever Father Brennan knocked on the door. Jill hadn't been baptized yet in the Catholic Church—and she never was, because these events of February 1963 occurred before that could happen. They had plans for her parents, Iris Marie Johnson and Abraham Zebrak, to be married in the church, and all of them to be baptized. After that would come First Communions for Leo and Jill. And Iris. The rules and the rituals suited Jill fine; whenever Father Brennan was about to leave the house, she dropped in showy piety to her knees when he blessed them. That grated on Iris—as if she knew Jill better than Jill knew herself.

Cattle huddled together, their eyes iced over. The weather was violent, the house pummeled by snow, wind like a steel splitting wedge. In the worst of it, Jill was not allowed to go outside to fetch firewood for fear she might be buried by it. A boy up the canyon had lost his way in the snow, returning from the horse barn; by the time they found him he was hypothermic. He shivered so hard he cracked a tooth, and he could not say that it was Christmas Eve. To warm his body, his mother and father got naked with him into a feather bed. They fed him chicken broth and candy canes. To no avail. No one cleaned out his 6th grade school desk. They were in alphabetical order—his last name was Winski—and Jill's desk was behind his, near the cloakroom; a rank odor persisted—a half-eaten sandwich or perhaps simply the smell of boy, mud, snakeskin, and wet corduroy.

On the wall calendar, sweethearts smooched over an ice cream soda with two straws. At the kitchen table: red and cream velvet scraps, paper doilies. Glitter. Glue. Jill cut out red paper hearts. At the other end of the table, Papa slapped down playing cards, an impatient game of solitaire. Iris—Jill has called her mother by her first name since that time and Iris does not correct her—Iris rocked Dan, a hot water bottle wrapped in flannel against his ear. He whimpered. In overalls, Sissy played on the floor. From the pantry, a basketball game broadcast through static. Leo was in there on a stool, his neck bent to the radio. Their grizzled dog Fisher moaned in dog dreams.

They were together.

Even if it was a hard winter.

Earlier in the day, Jill had seen Papa walk up behind Iris at the stove and put his arms around her waist and lay his head on her shoulder. She had kissed his cheek. Jill's face turned red at such moments, just as it did when people kissed chastely in movies. Most movie kisses were chaste in those days. But still embarrassing. Even now Jill cannot bear to watch romantic movies with anyone else present. There's a name for how she feels: asexual. But then nobody parsed these things. She might have been called an old maid then or spinster.

Almost whispering, Iris began to sing. *On a hill far away. Stood an old rugged cross.*

"That's a Protestant song," Papa said, a cautious edge to his voice.

Jill eyed them warily, the scissors at rest, mid-cut in the red construction paper. Iris shifted Dan's weight in her arms. He was four years old, lanky-limbed already, and people said he would be tall like Papa. His face was as white as the inside of an apple. He sucked his thumb.

Gently Iris said, "I might be Catholic soon, but I'll always have those songs in my head." She had been baptized by a holy roller, Papa called him, in a frost-cold river, when she was twelve; there is a photo of her shivering right after—a white cotton garment plastered against her body, shoulders hunched as if to shield her budding breasts, her mouth open in a dark O.

The basketball game ended in a roar. Leo switched it off. He came out of the pantry, swatting an extra pair of socks against his thigh. He sat down and pulled on the socks. "I'm going," he said.

"Going where?" Iris asked.

"To town."

Before Iris could say that it was too cold or too dangerous, Papa said, "Let him go."

Leo went to the door and hopped around, getting into his boots. "I have to see Lisbeth." He kissed Iris's cheek. She closed her eyes and stuck out her jaw, as if enduring the kiss. She fished out a seed catalog from a pile on the end table; she stared at that catalog cover as if vexation could make tomatoes grow.

"You don't get a ride in fifteen minutes," Papa instructed, "come in and warm up."

That was the last moment they were all together. Sissy on the floor in overalls, pounding colored pegs into a board with a wooden hammer. Dan sick with the earache. Leo running off to his girlfriend. Papa restless. Iris swoll up like a toad, Papa would've said if he hadn't wanted something from her. "Nice," Leo said to Jill, about the valentines.

The door clapped shut when he went out, startling Dan; he flailed in Iris's arms. The room took a few minutes to recover its heat. The mica window on the wood stove glowed with what Jill thought of as hellfire. She believed all the Bible stories then. They all did. It took decades of reading to make her understand that those stories are just stories, but they're still important.

As for God, she weaned herself from God in her twenties. People she knew, oldsters like herself, were going back to church. They got close to dying and they wanted the comfort of it. But she didn't have time for church, and she couldn't abide reciting words and praise aloud that defied science. On a Saturday evening or Sunday morning, she might have been talking to the orchard workers, pressing envelopes of cash into their callused hands, or spraying her trees and fruit. She was a crone. No permed hair. Not ugly or cruel. More the wise woman crone, in her better moments. When others turned to God, she turned to herself. When you are twelve and your life disintegrates, one choice you have is to turn inward and that is what she chose. It had been a lonely life that eventually became mere solitude. Even that word was too grand for the way she lived.

That bitter cold night in 1963, her fingers were sticky with paste; she pressed a paper doily onto a heart. "I'll hitch to town when I'm as old as Leo." She knew it was the wrong thing to say if she wanted to keep the peace. Back then she had that fighting instinct, just like Iris. Always saying the one true thing likely to cause upset.

Papa said, "You got another thing comin'."

"We did," Iris said. "In Baltimore."

"That was wartime," Papa shot back.

He scraped his chair back from the table; his boots knocked on the floor; his shadow crossed over Jill's valentines. He went to the front window, cuffed back the curtain, and she imagined that he watched Leo and wished that he, too, were headed into the unknown.

Jill didn't know if Papa ever grew out of his own adolescence; a kind of recklessness governed him; ill-advised decisions would haunt him all his life. She wasn't sure she loved him; whatever there was between them felt too often like tug-of-war. Could she break down that word love into the songs he played on his mouth harp? The memory of tobogganing down steep hills with him holding her tight? The way, when she paid a visit to his dwelling, he respectfully poured her a glass of High Ten? Acknowledgement of what she had become: solvent, owner of an orchard, a businesswoman.

"We repaired ships," Iris said, her voice laced with defiance, and something else: wonder. "I had a job repairing ships." Then: "We worked around the clock. If you were on night shift, you went out dancing in the morning. You hot-bedded it with another girl. She slept in your bed at night. You slept in it after you went out dancing."

His back to them, Papa said, "Iris, honey?" And Jill thought: Here it comes.

Iris glanced up at him, suspicious of that *honey*.

Oh, how she wanted them to love each other. To make a safe place for her. And if Jill's younger life had been a search for anything, it was for a safe place created by love. But the currency of adult love was sex, and she could not muster more than passing interest in it.

"Olds Carver says summer sausage's ready. That'd taste good tonight, wouldn't it?"

"And what'd you lose last time?"

Dan began to wail, his nose snotty. Iris reached for a worn diaper, so thin you could see through it. She had a cache of worn-out clothes she washed and folded and used for rags. That was Iris: frugal to the bone. As if to amend for Papa's spendthrift habits. Once he bought her a new coat—a wine-colored wool coat with silver buttons—and she made him take it back to the store.

"I'm feeling lucky."

Iris's eyes drilled into him; she pursed her lips.

Papa said to Sissy: "Want to go with Papa?" He held out his arms to her. "'Member Louise? You can play with Louise."

Given the weather, and the way winter afternoons were cut short by night, Jill did not think Iris would agree to that.

"Don't take more than ten dollars," she said. If she argued with herself about letting Sissy go, you couldn't tell. It was a plain equation: if Papa took Sissy, he wouldn't stay up the canyon indefinitely. A logger, he was laid off for the winter. When Jill can coax Iris to look back on those times, she would say, "He'd go out for milk and be gone for a week."

Dan fell asleep on the sofa, his fever down. Iris went into her bedroom and came out wearing fake pearl earrings and lipstick and a clean chamois shirt. Jill stacked her valentines on the kitchen counter. She had the not unreasonable worry that Iris might leave her there with Dan and go out to the Slabtown Tavern a few streets over. Women now call what Iris had done "self-care"—primping a bit, putting on earrings, just to stay at home. She offered to make popcorn; when that was ready, they sat talking at the kitchen table. Iris repeated what was on her mind: Jill shouldn't get in trouble, that her friend Elise would be one to get in trouble, that Leo was too young to be running off to town to see his girlfriend, that she wanted Jill to remember the Ten Commandments and that she herself had taught Jill the Ten Commandments. She drank a glass of beer and told her these things; all Jill had to do was meet her eyes and she would go on. But Jill looked at her cross-eyed when she said that about Elise. "Don't talk back," Iris warned. The waiting—for Papa and Sissy—was like a sore tooth your tongue flicks over.

A siren cut into the house. It might've cut into every house for miles around. Iris padded to the kitchen window; she ran cold water over her cigarette butt. "What in the world . . ."

"A fire?" House fires were not unusual in the winter. Pajamas might catch fire when half-asleep you opened the wood stove to shove in another log. Or a spark might fly to a pile of old newspapers.

Jill's fingers felt oily from the popcorn; her body felt glued to the chair; she could not move to wipe her fingers. Iris went to the front window where a paper snowflake hung in each pane, taped crookedly. A knock rattled the back door. Fisher slunk to the door and growled.

"Someone's here, Mama," Jill said.

She said, "I see that."

Three things happened at once: the siren wound down, losing steam; Dan cried out in his sleep; and a knock shook the glass in the back window.

"Sheriff here, Mrs. Zebrak."

Her forehead gashed with worry lines, Iris commanded Fisher to settle down and opened the door a crack. "Yes?"

Jill could not hear what the sheriff said, but Iris backed off, crying, "Oh, God oh God oh Jesus . . ." She doubled over, gasping. The sirens screamed again. The sheriff pushed the door open, and Fisher ran out. Jill kept thinking what would make grownups leave a door wide open in the middle of winter. She thought of what they might say under other circumstances. Shut the goddamn door. Were you born in a barn?

"Everyone'll be up there," he said. "Looking."

Iris mashed her face with both hands. She pulled at her hair. "Let me think, let me think." She stared right through Jill, a fist against her mouth. Then: "We'll go. You go ahead. I'll get someone to stay with Dan. Dan's got an earache. I'll get someone to stay with him . . ." She marched to the telephone. "We'll be right behind you."

Tenderness and concern in his voice, the sheriff said, "Yes, ma'am. If that's what you want."

Iris said, "It's what I want."

The sheriff left, pulling the back door shut. It was only then Jill felt free to speak. But her body was cement heavy. "What's wrong?"

Iris's face was pale, winter-white, grainy; she pressed her forehead to the flowered wallpaper, as if she could melt into the house and it might give her refuge. She hammered the telephone receiver against the wall. "This'll kill me," she said.

"Is it Papa?"

She would not say. She telephoned the neighbor, Mrs. Bartlett, an old woman who sometimes watched Sissy and Dan in exchange for venison cuts. Jill put on her school coat and rubber boots. Iris opened a high linen closet and reached up for blankets. She yanked one down; a canvas bag of yarn tumbled out, and a litter of squealing baby mice fell from the bag, pink and hairless, half the length of wooden matches. Jill yelped and Iris shoved her hard. "Go, go!"

On the way to the car, they passed Mrs. Bartlett sweeping in, a wool scarf tied under her chin, a plate of food in hand. The cold took Jill's breath away. She could not look Mrs. Bartlett in the eye, as if she had done something shameful. That uncalled for shame—about family—is a feeling that stayed with her. A feeling she nodded to and shoved away. In the car, Iris drove and at the same time scraped the inside of the windshield. She tucked the window scraper between her legs. Jill's teeth chattered; the bald tires slipped in the snow.

Finally, Iris said, "It's Sissy."

"Sissy?"

"And Olds Carver's wife—Janet. She was bringing Sissy home."

"And Papa?" Jill asked.

"Papa's with Olds. Now don't talk to me. Say a prayer. Say it out loud. Say the Our Father."

As Jill prayed, Iris tugged her gloves off with her teeth and lit a cigarette. Her chapped hands trembled; her fingers were stained yellow with nicotine. "Son of a bitch," she would say. "This is a godforsaken place."

At the accident the slick road was lined with cars and pickups. The sheriff's truck was there, an empty boat trailer hooked to its rear end. Iris slid the car into an icy turnout at the northern end of a sharp curve, the grill abutting Papa's truck. Headlights and taillights had been left on; five warning flares the color of hunters' caps spit on the straightaway beyond. Snow fell down the riverbank in deep blue folds. Bare willows grew thick and tangled beyond the heaviest snow, then there were rocks and boulders, then the river, icy along the edge, but thawed in the middle, the swift, blackish water riffled. On the other bank, scraggly lodge pole pine grew in strict formation, the fearful woods of fairy tales.

"Stay here," Iris said. "Get under a blanket."

She threw open the car door and charged behind the car and down the riverbank in long strides, her coat open, her arms outstretched. She slipped twice, nearly falling. Papa came up to her and she fought him off, cursing him. At her darkest moment she cursed him. Finally, she let him help her down the slippery path until they were out of Jill's sight.

Ambulance headlights shone on the river. There were men and women in parkas and felt-pac boots strung out all along the river, bits of red or blue in the fading twilight. An aluminum boat bobbed on the water; the two men in the boat unsteadily poked a long pole under the ice shelves, their headlamps blinding Jill. Black slickers shined in the cut of the ambulance headlights.

Two women stomped their boots, their breath coming in great clouds, beside the car. One said, "That place needs a guardrail in the worst way." The other one said, "It wouldn't've made a difference. She had some momentum behind her."

Leo leaned into the car window, his hair frosted with snow. How did he know so soon? Jill never asked him. He reached in and took her hand. "Our sister's drowned," he said.

"No, she's not," Jill said.

He opened the car door and sat down on the edge of the seat, one boot in and one boot out. He put his arm around her. "Jill. This's the truth. Sissy's gone."

"Get away from me," she said.

He got out of the car and said, "There's a fire. Go get warmed up."

Jill forgot that Iris had told her to stay put. She got out into the night, and the night—the canyon, the chaos of the search—felt big, endless. She perched at the head of a tamped down path—glossy and hard—that led to the river. Someone yelled, "Hold on!" And another voice: "It's her . . ." Iris and Papa were visible beside a stack of boulders, their arms around each other, her face in his coat lapels. The moon had come up, silvering everything. Two river rescue men waded out and hauled a bulky body from the hook on the pike pole. They rolled her onto the rocky bank, losing purchase once, falling to their knees. "Lordy, Lordy, she's heavy."

Olds Carver bellowed with grief. Jill had not seen him, but his cry rolled around the canyon, and in it was the sum of his loss. People looked away.

That was the body of Janet Carver, but they did not find Sissy. They gave up looking, and that was not unusual in the winter. A body slips under the thick ice and there is nothing to do but wait it out, until spring thaw. They left the pickup there and Papa drove them home, with Iris crying out violently against the passenger window all the way. She kept on talking, but much of what she said was lost to sorrow, strangled in her throat. Jill understood this much: "You goddamn son-of-a-bitch." And: "That was my baby girl—mine, mine—do you hear me? She came out of *me* . . ."

Iris had a filigree friendship ring, given her by a woman she had met in Baltimore during the war—Mary Helen. They shared a room in a boarding house; Mary Helen was the woman she hot bedded with. It was a common practice. The shipyard had attracted more workers than the town could provide for. Sometimes the sheets would be infected with scabies and the mites would drive a woman to distraction. But Iris said that Mary Helen and she were ever vigilant; they had one set of sheets and washed them in scalding hot water once a week and hung them out to dry in the wind.

Helen was Jill's middle name.

Singing was one of the few ways a woman of that time might distinguish herself; good girls with good voices sang in the choir; if she were what Aunt Mina called cheap, she might sing in dive-bars. But during the war there had been a middle ground, and Mary Helen and Iris would get up before a microphone at the dances and sing a Kitty Kallen tune, with fake flowers in their hair. They loved to dance and there were dances around the clock, in dance pavilions, on the decks of ships, and in church basements. Later, when Jill was a child, if Tommy Dorsey or Jack Teagarden would come on the radio or television, Iris would get up and dance by herself across the linoleum. Papa was not a dancer. When she talked about those times somehow Jill pictured her mother and Mary Helen dancing together. She knew that the ring had to mean something. She wanted to wear it. She begged her for it. One day Iris said that Jill could wear it to school. She was not to take it off all day. And of course she lost it. She was ten years old. She cannot remember taking it off, but she did not have it when she returned home. And Iris wept at the table later that night, after Papa had gone out. She tried to hide it, but her face was red and raw as flesh stung by nettles.

The only time Jill had seen her worse off was when Sissy drowned.

The house was full of people; it was near midnight.

Aunt Mina was in the kitchen, doing up the dishes they had left in the sink. Her hair was completely white and long and thin, and she wore it in a braid pinned into a bun at the nape of her neck; her scalp was pink as taffy. Aunt Mina had been a waitress in a beer garden in Prague when she was young, before her father committed suicide, before her mother packed up all the children and came in steerage to the New World; Jill had seen a stiff sepia photo of her with a tray aloft, smiling.

Father Brennan was at the kitchen table, a shiny bottle of whiskey open before him. Jill was certain Aunt Mina did not approve of that; you could feel it in the haughty way she held her shoulders.

Iris's friend Madge and her husband Bud sat in the living room, smoking, with their coats on. No one had built up the fire. Leo went directly to the wood stove and knelt down and got the fire blazing.

"I can't face anyone," Iris said, to no one in particular.

Mrs. Bartlett resolutely put on her coat. She patted Iris's shoulder on her way out.

"Don't do that," Iris said to Aunt Mina, who froze at the sink. They had a longstanding battle over housework. Aunt Mina pitched in, unasked, whenever she came to their house, and Iris took it as criticism.

Father Brennan had poured Papa a glass of whiskey.

"Get—out—of—here," Iris bawled. And to make her point, she went to the oak table and dumped everything on the floor: the whiskey bottle, glasses, car keys, a cigar box full of crayons, a teapot of dollar bills and loose change. Father Brennan started up and backed against the wall as if he might be injured. Papa lunged at Iris, grabbing her neck. Leo jumped on his back. Jill cringed against the wall, hiding her eyes.

Everyone packed up and left. Dan was carried out to Father Brennan's station wagon in a blanket, and he went to town to stay with Aunt Mina and he never returned home. At times like that you make adjustments; decisions are made that seem temporary, and yet a life turns on the moment.

Jill went to the window and peered out at the snow; her left hip ached, that old icepick pain. It would go away when she started moving around. The temperature had dropped, and the sleet had turned to fat flakes blown about by the wind. She needed gas in her car. She needed to check the tire pressure. She'd been considering buying new tires before winter came on in full force; that time might be now. Or soon. She pictured the different routes to Pittsburgh. The one she enjoyed seemed out of the question, taking all day to meander through the small towns along the Monongahela River. What she enjoyed would not matter now. She had to be dependable. She had prided herself on always being there for Harper. Harper's mother had long ago left the family for a doctor in Savannah she had met on a Bahamian vacation with girlfriends. Out by the road, Papa stood with Adele Pratt while she waited for her ride. He wasn't dressed for the weather, except for an earflap hat. His hands were bare. He had one arm around Adele, holding her head against his chest, as if to keep her warm, and in the other hand, he pinched a lit cigarette between his thumb and forefinger. He wore house slippers on his feet.

She went into her bedroom and started packing. Braeburn came after her quizzically, asking for breakfast. She fed him and let him out. For some unknown reason she had done so much laundry two days before that nearly everything she owned was clean. This was the reason why. She packed without thinking. Corduroys, sweaters, winter socks. She would wear her hiking boots. There was a thirty-pound bag of dog food in the car. The dog would come along to Pittsburgh. She didn't want to ask him for anything now.

When Papa came in, she told him about Harper.

"Is she okay?"

"Apparently not. But she's alive."

He poured himself a cup of coffee and sat down at the kitchen table. "That's bad news."

"I want you to leave for a while."

"Me?"

"Yes. I want you to find another place to stay."

"Are you serious?"

"I am."

"If this's about Adele…"

"It's not, really." She thought about how inconvenient conflict had always seemed to her. But she had to plow on into it. "I want your place for Harper. She's going to need a place to recover."

"Where'm I going to go?"

"Go stay at Adele's. They've got lots of rooms there. You're not asking for charity. You can afford to pay them something."

"Who's going to haul in those bags of dog food for you?"

"There's always someone who wants to help an old woman."

He did his version of storming out. He rooted around in the cupboard until he found a stainless-steel go-cup. He poured his coffee into it and set the ceramic mug down too hard in the sink. It made a cracking sound. Out he went into what was becoming the first snowstorm of winter. He slammed the back door, and the window glass over the sink quivered.

That's how Abraham Zebrak came to live at the Tansy Art Dispensary on the edge of Whistle Pig. He could walk everywhere. Some of his youthful vigor returned, living among women. He shaved every other day and dabbed on the Pinaud Clubman. Adele cut his hair regularly—he still had a shock of unruly white hair. He looked after Adele Pratt and the other women who lived there, all artists, supposedly, Jill would think dismissively. He hauled in bags of clay for the potters. He fetched packages of supplies ordered at the art store in Cumberland. Jill thought she would never speak to him again. It was age-old rancor, like a scar on her body that throbbed in certain kinds of weather. Harper shuttled back and forth between the Tansy and the orchard, bringing news of her great-grandfather, gossip, really, tidbits of this or that, and Jill would not dignify them with discussion. She never talked about Papa—everyone in Whistle Pig called him Papa now. Doug broke up with Harper when he saw what had become of her left hand and foot. Crushed beyond repair. Harper wore a T-shirt with a positive slogan about disabilities. She liked to say that some relationships have expiration dates, an expression she learned from a late-night comic. It was something Iris might say. That was it, Jill would think. A rational cynicism being their philosophy from then on out.

Truer Words

Once a week Harper borrowed Aunt Jill's car and took her great-grandfather Papa to the casino. She knew nothing of casinos, even though she'd once been to Las Vegas. The first time, Papa escorted her to the booth where she was given a guest pass like a credit card with seven gratis dollars on it. She chose a purple lanyard and slipped it around her neck. While he planted himself in front of the poker machines, she made quick work of the seven dollars at the slots. She won twenty-one dollars and decided to keep it. At his habitual poker machine Papa kept a hungry eye on the bartender, a woman in makeup like a mask, her eyes overboard smoky. He bought Harper a margarita that tasted like lighter fluid. Not that she knew what lighter fluid tasted like, but it was raw low-shelf tequila, the worst. "You need more practice, gal," he said, laughing that croaky elderly laugh. Maniacal was a word to put to it. Same old, same old. Every week.

In the ambulance she had said, "My cleaning rags are clean and folded." The EMT told her this later. She had also said, "You're hot, you know." He tracked her down, which must have been against the rules. He told her what she was like after the accident. He said she was lucky to have only one scar on her face, a pinkish crescent on her cheekbone the size of a clipped thumbnail. She had a beautiful face, he said, perhaps reciprocity for telling him he was hot. She didn't trust anyone now. It crossed her mind in the ambulance that her mother might be waiting at the hospital; then she remembered that her mother was in India.

Her hand was crushed. Obliterated. The engagement ring wasn't even there any longer, and she had to consider that a sign from the universe: Doug backing out was inevitable. After considerable prodding, he said that he didn't want to be married to someone handicapped. She told him to say disabled. He said, Come *on*.

Oh, there were other reasons. The usual. He applied for a job in Phoenix and needed the time and space to adjust to that. Experience had taught him that it was hard to maintain a long-distance relationship. He was a few years older and could always use "experience" to justify anything.

One time during the initial separation she sprang for a cheap casino airline ticket from Pittsburgh to Las Vegas, and they met in a hotel that had a 24-hour buffet with latkes and smoked salmon. That's all she wanted, latkes. They seemed homey among the bright lights. Doug wanted to see strippers. He read to her from one club's website: advice to couples. She had shrieked: *abso-fucking-lutely* not. She couldn't see herself being touched by other women, strippers, younger women who had not been obliterated.

He had said, "But what about…"

She put up her hand like a stop sign. He was about to bring up the time they went to a strip club in Pittsburgh, a place where the dancers had tattoos on the backs of their thighs. She had wanted to go. She had been what he called an eager beaver. And she didn't think there was anything wrong with being teased like that. She liked the camaraderie with him, the forbidden feel, the two of them mainlining lust.

In Las Vegas, when he came back, he wanted sex. But he went limp. He went limp when she touched him with what was left of her crushed hand. Now she looks back and marvels at how willing she was for so long.

She could do all kinds of things with what was left of her crushed hand, even though it ached like hell, especially at night. A doctor prescribed Gabapentin so that she could sleep pain-free, a medication with many uses she discovered online. They gave it to humans and animals for anxiety. They said it was not addictive. Around eight o'clock every night she looked forward to taking it, and it crossed her mind that it may not be addictive, but it was certainly habit-forming. She slept peacefully, and her obliterated hand did not ache until about four the next afternoon. It was a handy medication, she told herself and laughed—a guttural grunt—at the word handy.

Things she could do with her obliterated left hand included masturbating—letting off steam or steamin', as she had called it since high school—and shoving wood into the wood stove. With her two remaining fingers, she could thin apples during thinning season and keep her balance on a ladder. For everything else she relied mostly on her right hand. Texting required training herself to use only one thumb. One foot was messed up, too, and learning to ride a bike again had been tricky. She finally asked her dad to buy her a recumbent bike, and that alleviated the fear of losing her balance.

Living with Aunt Jill was easy-peasy.

After a month in the house with Aunt Jill, she took the offer to make the shed/shop/Papa's house her own. Papa had moved into Whistle Pig, into an artists' co-op. She was tired of the way she and Jill could not settle on what to call Papa's place, so she gave it an official name, like a resort cabin—Early Bird. They had a wooden sign made to that effect. She had found reasons to contact the woodworker in Durango via Etsy during the design stage. And after it arrived, she thanked him twice. Once she sent him a photo of the Early Bird sign she thought he might use in marketing. In the photo she is standing beside the Early Bird in her most outdoor-aficionado clothing, figuring a guy in Durango would go for that. A wool sweater. Hiking boots. Her hair—her glory—around her shoulders, lifted in tendrils by the breeze on the ridge. Then she woke up one morning chastising herself for a crush on a man she did not know, did not live nearby, and who might be an abuser or dangerous in some yet to be imagined way. His photo on Etsy might have been fake. She never wrote to him again.

The Early Bird was one room, 20 x 20, finished inside with salvaged barn board, silvery and rough, so that when she woke up, if the sun were coming in at just the right slant, she felt as if she were inside a cloud being cut into by sunlight. She felt contented. Satisfied. Well-being that had been hers as a girl, that is, until her mother left. Then she would realize, my hand, my foot, and sometimes she would get pissed. The old Why Me pity would beckon her like a siren song. When that happened, she had to get up, start a fire, brew pour-over coffee, a special coffee she ordered from a roaster in Harrisburg, and she would check the weather, read the PG online, and then do yoga on a bright red mat. Her silicone great toe prosthetic made it possible to do yoga poses. *Stay busy* was her mantra. Routine was good. That's why she liked taking Papa to the casino.

There was a bar in Whistle Pig that catered to grown-ups. Students from the college in Riley went to a different bar, Wild Thing, and she had heard that after closing there were sometimes fights outside Wild Thing, and sometimes couples who had no other place to go would have sex in the deep vestibule of a derelict building across the street. You might see a discarded condom on the sidewalk the next day. She avoided Wild Thing after trying it once. The postgrad bar was called Spooner's, in honor of one of William S. Burrough's cats. Inside Spooner's were posters of 20th century writers the owners adored. They were former English majors who moved to the mountains for college and never left. Harper liked to sit at the inside end of the bar, far from the door, arriving early, to watch the conviviality begin as drinkers swooped in. She liked to think of them swooping in. When she was part of a college crowd—almost ten years ago—they called going out drinking *swooping*. At Spooner's most people stood in the skinny gap between the bar and the wall. It was tight. And roaring, once past the first round or two. She liked to watch the way men and women—gay, straight, non-binary, trans, and possibly aces, like Aunt Jill—squeezed past each other, brushing bodies. This was before Covid when people breathed all over each other, kissed each other. It was ecstatic. It was almost orgiastic. And hopeful.

She met Jack Norman at Spooner's. A painter. His clothes spattered with his current palette, sandals on his tanned feet, his hair in a tangled golden wave that covered one eye. He would push it back and give you his perfected riveting stare. Blue eyes the color of the sea at the best beaches. He smoked. Nobody's perfect. He would go out to the patio. The second time he asked her to go along. He rolled a cigarette, licking the paper with a delicate tongue maneuver that seemed feral. Out there, in the fading daylight, she saw that his hair was shot through with silver and he was missing one tooth, an eye tooth. The smell of dog shit rose over the shadowbox fence. Music from the American Legion came at them: *Shake it for the young bucks sittin' in the honky-tonks*. Try as she might to ignore it, the images in the song hammered away at her, distracted her. That's the kind of place this is. Whistle Pig, she meant. Inside they were listening to Blind Faith, totally retro, but she didn't think the people in Spooner's saw it that way. Irony seemed in short supply.

He wanted to paint her. She didn't trust him, but she said okay. Maybe sometime.

"Now!"

It had been a long time since a man insisted on his way with her. Her inner feminist said, What the hell. Don't boss me around. But she asked, "Now?"

"I like to paint at night."

"Where?"

She was sitting on the picnic table bench beside him, her legs on either side of the bench, which suddenly struck her as flirtatious. He reached over and put his hands on her hips and squeezed. "It's not far," he said. "I walked."

She got up and followed him out the creaking back gate into the town parking lot. Her recumbent bike would be safe, locked to a stout iron ring embedded in a stone that must have at one time—150 years ago—been used to tie up a horse. A little fountain was lit up with colored lights under the water. In an upstairs apartment someone practiced playing a trumpet. There was the smell of garlic, the smell of bread baking. That indefatigable dog shit smell. Her senses felt finely tuned. He took her hand, her perfect hand. She tried not to limp. After a block, she said, "My foot's injured. I have to slow down."

She'd been up this alley before. It led to Hart Street, the highest point on the western edge of town. After that it was all woods and Moose Lodge. Bears probably chose this route to lumber in and raid the garbage cans.

In the full summer dark, a small boy whizzed down the alley on a scooter. He stopped and said, "Hi, Jack."

Jack stopped and mussed his hair and said, "Hi, Buddy."

The boy asked, "Who's that?"

"Harper." The way he said it sounded like a door closing.

"Okay." The boy made a sputtering noise with his lips, as if on a dirt bike, one sneaker foot slapping the blacktop to get going.

"Adios," Jack said.

"Adios," the boy hollered.

Once she had gone to France. She and Doug had walked out the little dappled road to Cezanne's studio, with its rosy gate and shutters, where the walls gave off the scent of linseed oil and Cezanne's bowler was sitting there on the mantel. She wondered whether the staff replenished the scent of linseed oil, but she also felt enchanted.

Jack's studio engendered a similar enchantment: the stainless-steel cart on wheels filled to overflowing with tubes of paint, most of them squished, the gloomy paintings leaning against the wall, the industrial chandelier, the brocade sofa with its shiny worn spots, and the single bed shoved up against the wall, its linens rumpled. The place smelled like weed. Overpoweringly.

The walls were studded with crosses, the crosses ornamented with flotsam, bits of trash. "You're not . . . one of those very, very religious people, are you?" she asked. "Lots of those around here."

"'You behold in me a horrible example of free thought.'"

"Ulysses!"

"You're a smart one."

Clearly, she was one of many. Women he wanted to paint.

He was letting her in on a secret place. For that, she let him run his hands up under her shirt. She was glad she wasn't wearing a bra. While he did that she asked, "You live here?" It seemed there was no bathroom; it was a pertinent question. He ran his thumbs over her nipples and said, "No questions. That's not the way to get to know me."

He was one of those men who wouldn't even tell you his favorite band. As if they put you on a diet and doled out tiny bits of information about themselves to keep you always keen for more. They were training you like a bird dog. She hated that. They were pathologically private. She had noticed a trend in herself: She generalized about men. Was it fair? Probably not. But statements about men would burble up in her mind on their own as if she could not control her assessments. They felt like received knowledge from generations of women.

But those thumbs, the deft way he turned off the overhead while guiding her to the bed.

When she showed him her obliterated hand in the dark, he kissed her pinky, licked her pinky, and sweetly said, "Ah, a defect." She felt a rush of vulnerability when he said that. She was too grateful for it. She knew that. But it felt good. When was the last time she had felt this kind of good?

Outside, there was the hollow bam-bam-bam of a dribbling basketball, distracting her from the business at hand.

"You'll get used to it."

"What makes you think I'll be back?"

"You'll be back."

Afterwards, she almost tiptoed down the wooden steps and out into the alley. Houses were bright with the evening solace of lamps in every window, miniature domestic dramas she did not have to understand. Still, her mind went there: terse exchanges, or a child being smacked with a wooden spoon, or a mother leaving for good. When she got to that one, it felt like a slug to her solar plexus. There were entirely too many meannesses ongoing. She pictured a faux-frontier tavern near Hoover Dam she and Doug had driven to the day after the stripper conflict. It was designed to seem like another country, a poorer country, Doug said, a place of unaccountable cheer and trepidation. The decrepit jukebox played only two songs, a song of leaving and a song of love. People entering were told to place their weapons in a lard can on the counter. Put your fucking weapons down, she told him. And he laughed.

There were ruts in the gravel where she imagined Jack's car was usually parked. Or someone's car. The moon was up, like the inside of the French melons in Aunt Jill's garden, that orange. She could not guess the time. Nearby, a dog barked half-heartedly. Propelled by a spree of hormones, she scooted past the backside of the funeral home when out the corner of one eye she sensed movement; she could not stop herself from glancing toward the brick building. The garage doors were open wide, the interior lit with a bluish florescent strip. A white sheet or blanket like a flag of surrender covered a table or gurney. Who washed their sheets and blankets? How did they keep them so glaringly white? Without rubbernecking she could not tell if there was a body underneath. The funeral director, a lithe blond woman, was at the ready. This seemed to say that women were taking over. She tried to imagine the blond woman lifting a heavy body. She tried to imagine the woman lifting her body, had she died in the crash. You could depend on a woman to do that, she thought, dragging her foot onward. She waved, but the woman was busy, walking out to greet two men who had arrived in a silver truck.

He had said he would text her about when to come back; he would start the preliminary sketches.

She felt the kind of exuberance that made her want to do something nice for someone. There was the liquor store lit up like a Christmas tree in the otherwise small-town gloom of a side street. She went inside the door with the filthy metal handle, the handprints of so many people, possibly obliterated people, the glass door plastered with wrinkled photocopies of the faces of shoplifters, and a crookedly hand-lettered sign refusing service to those fiends. The liquor store lights were bright like the lights of an operating room. The doctors and nurses had been joking about Trump. She hadn't been able to laugh because of the plastic unit over her face. A thumbs-up with her good hand was all she had in her and then, whoosh, she was out.

At the counter she bought two Ravens lottery tickets.

The woman at the register asked, "Is that all, hon?"

"Yep," she said. The guy in front of her had said, "Yep," so she did, too. When in Rome.

And she charged out of there before anyone could notice her or speak to her. She gave off the whiff of sex. A shower, shower, my soul for a shower.

Lottery tickets brought to mind her mother. When she went in the liquor store for a bottle of wine, she would come out with two tickets, and Harper would scratch off the numbers. They once won five hundred dollars. They split it. Harper spent her half on clothes. Every spring her mother would take her shopping for summer nightgowns and sandals. After that, they would have lunch, but not at the food court of some down-at-the-heels mall. They would go to Squirrel Hill and have kebabs or samosas. Her mother would let her have a sip of wine. The mother memes, she called these images. They cycled through. She had gotten to the point where the mother memes no longer made her sad. Or the sadness was a thin membrane under the muscle of love. She could remember and be glad she had those times. Times of Mother.

With halting gait, she walked to the Tansy, texted Papa, and in a half-minute he came down the steep stone steps, one gnarly hand gripping the handrail, his old man knees angled out.

She gave him the scratch-offs. He was delighted to receive them and delighted to see her. He offered a sip of whiskey from a half-pint bottle. But she wrinkled her nose in distaste.

"Girlie?"

What's with hon and girlie? "Yep?"

"How're you gettin' back home?"

"My bike's at Spooner's."

Under his breath Papa said, "Goddamnit." He drew a shiny quarter from his pants pocket.

The front windows of the Tansy were open, and Edith Piaf spilled out, as if Piaf herself were tripping down to the sidewalk. The women inside squawked with laughter.

His fingernails were thick and bruised. The motion he made to scratch off the tickets was like whittling a sharp point on a stick for roasting marshmallows. He'd done that for her, in the long ago.

She said, "I'm okay."

A woman with long gray hair at the window said, "Come on in. You, too, Harper. How about a game of rummy?"

What would it be like to go in? She had never. She would be giving in to something. A different stage of life. The women, their grandkids. The music they played, the booze they drank. She could imagine it: the hours they kept, someone always up, a pot of coffee perking at three in the morning, the buzzing light in the kitchen blue on the leftovers. Their flabby arms embracing her. It was a life with no autonomy. She was only thirty. Thirty.

He tossed the spent tickets in the grass.

She asked, "Nothing?"

"Nope."

Harper retrieved the tickets. Humbly, humbly. She didn't want him littering but she didn't want to scold him, either.

"I betcha I could borrow a car."

"Nah, my bike's at the bar, I told you."

Papa leaned over and put his dry lips to her forehead. "Take care of your sweet self."

That's why she came. To have someone say what he had said.

When she wasn't with Jack she wondered why she went. He was an outlier among men in her life. She had always gravitated to men with closets full of dress shirts. Men who rose early to go to the gym and tackle the day. They used that word *tackle*. She had worked as an underling at a non-profit arts agency; she'd worn slightly edgy business wear. When she and the men met up for drinks after work, she felt they were a matched set, even if she was a little more unconventional.

It was not comfortable in Jack's studio unless she were in the single bed with all the lights dim. With one bright light aimed at his sketch, he worked; she sat in bed without her clothes, earbuds in, listening to podcasts. She liked "She's All Fat." Not that she had ever been fat, but she wanted to hear all the body positivity messages, and she needed to ignore the unpleasant aspects of his domesticity. To pee she had to go out in the dark to the jungle under an ancient shaggy wisteria vine. Bourbon was all he had to drink. She had suggested an electric kettle for tea, but he said, "Don't start trying to civilize me, Zeebie." Zeebie was his nickname for her; her last name was Zebrak. He would text about an hour before he wanted her there. It was always the same time. Around nine. Summer dusk. When hidden lives unfold in a wash of blue and night. They never discussed it, but she instinctively knew not to come at any other time. He'd probably be painting. She wondered why she went, but once she was peddling up the alley, she knew why she went or thought she knew. She could feel her pelvis opening like a flower, like a blood-red peony. Her pelvis, and then her vulva. He knew what to do to open her up.

After the sex, she didn't want to be there. That seemed to be a thought she had ignored most of her life, particularly with boys, and then, with men. You kept on pushing down the thought because they might give you something you wanted. After a while, she would forget about not wanting to be there. That's how far she was from what she really wanted.

Afterwards, too, she felt risky. Energized by heart-thudding sex, she rode her bike up and down Brick Mountain in the dark, by the gleam of the moon when it was out, or by icy cones of light emitted from a tangle of battery-run units she had attached at various points on the bike.

Back home at the orchard, during the day, she usually spent a couple hours helping Aunt Jill repair field crates, in anticipation of the fall harvest. In a goofy-looking sunhat she slathered on Japanese sunscreen. Then they would drink quarts of herbal iced tea. It was the lull between thinning and picking, a July so hot she felt feverish if she stayed in the sun too long. Aunt Jill asked: "Why're you going to town so much?" And she asked: "There's this guy." Aunt Jill said: "Don't give your heart away. So soon, I mean." Harper laughed and asked: "What kind of fool do you take me for?"

One night while they slept, a black bear tore up the bee boxes. The next morning two men from the DNR showed up with their pellet guns and sardines. They seduced the bear into a crate with sardines. When they let her go, one peppered her rump with rubber shot, and the other one—the handsome one—set off fireworks. Harper noted that he was good-looking in a Robert Pattison kind of way, with long lashes and eyebrows that participated when he frowned, but she did not leap to wondering if she might attract him.

That's when she knew that Jack had a claim on her. It seemed to go back to that moment when he licked her pinky and said, "Ah, a defect." It exhausted her to think about how she would have to reveal her defects to subsequent lovers. Do you allow a new man to discover your scars, the indentation on your right knee from stabbing yourself with an ice ax on a hiking trip in the Rockies, the crater on the bottom of your foot from stepping on a nail when you were nine, the long trail of pink-white skin on your forearm left there by a cousin's fingernail during an argument? The loss of her big toe in the accident? Or do you whisper the litany of scars to him? A let's-get-it-over-with strategy.

This went on for a few weeks. She loved the dense stand of sweet pea casting itself against his cedar fence. She loved the basketball players in the twilit alley, their dribbles against the asphalt. Whenever she slipped out of the studio they might still be there, sweaty boys drinking from plastic bottles. They gave her the once-over.

Doug liked pick-up games at the court near their apartment.

Doug liked anal.
Doug did not believe in celebrating Valentine's Day.
Doug knew how to make a mean martini. Any kind.
Doug used to bring her mango tea in bed.
Doug once bought her a black teddy.
Doug always took her car to Get-Go and filled up the tank when she needed gas. The obliterated car.

Would she ever stop thinking Doug-this, Doug-that?

She stopped when Jack was inside of her. Aunt Jill said that eventually she would stop thinking about sex all the time. That sounded cheerless.

She found the puppy beside the orchard sign, in among some chicory. He was brown all over except for a lopsided white circle around one eye. A designer dog, she called him. One of a kind.

He fit snugly into a sling she made out of a scarf she never wore anymore. His brown fur seemed cozy surrounded by the plaid scarf. Jack not wanting her to come unannounced went out the window. She talked to the dog: *Forget whoever dumped you, let's never think of them, let's be the best of friends.* She liked the way her voice shifted when she talked to the puppy, as if to a baby. Her recumbent bike flew into town and up the alley; it was a breezy day of petite clouds rippling above the blue metal roofs on Jack's block.

A rusted-out VW van was parked in the gravel behind the studio, its backside plastered with peeling bumper stickers. Only one stood out to her: *It will be a great day when schools get all the money they need and the Air Force has to hold a bake sale to buy a bomber.* She was down with that. The gate ka-chunked; that might let him know she was there. His lover, her puppy. That's how she felt, as if it were a solid world, with safety, bonding. Her new life.

Inside there was a woman—tall, rawboned, brown-eyed, in a stylish dress like a retro-peasant might wear. The hem of the dress was stained with wine or juice. Sunglasses perched above her forehead. She sorted through the paintings that had always been leaning against the wall. "Hi, there," she said. A baby in a T-shirt and diaper clung to the woman. When the baby noticed Harper, it whimpered and struck the woman's head with a pacifier. Another child peeked from behind the woman's skirt.

"That's Harper," he said. He was the boy who rode his scooter in the alley.

"Come on in," the woman said. She sat down, and with some adept magical adjustment of her bodice she began to nurse the baby, who smiled around the nipple. "Come on, it's okay."

"It's okay," the boy said, and he took Harper's hand and walked her to the chair that Jack sat on while he sketched and painted. She did as she was told; she sat. She put the puppy on the floor. The boy gently held her hand. The puppy peed on the floor, a surprisingly loud stream that turned the wooden floor a coffee brown.

"Oh, I'm sorry," Harper said.

The boy laughed. "My sister does that sometimes."

"It's cool," the woman said. "Nathan, here. Wipe that up."

The boy took the cloth she offered him and did a fair job of mopping up the pee. He set the cloth by the door and went to sit by the puppy and pet him; the puppy almost immediately climbed into the boy's lap. A Kodak moment.

The woman said, "I'm Lulu." Then: "I've seen you at the casino with Papa."

Harper frowned. "He's my great-grandfather."

"You might not recognize me without my makeup. My bartender's mask."

"Oh, my god," Harper said. "It's you."

"I've got nine lives." This came out like a dare.

A total non sequitur. Or was it?

"He probably let you think he went to art school, didn't he? He does that. Norm's a natural. His daddy worked in the mine where we grew up. He wanted Norm to go to school. To learn something that'd stand him in good stead when times got rough." She switched the baby to the other breast. "And his daddy said that's one thing you could be sure of. Times would get rough. But all Norm wanted to do was draw. First cars, then women."

Harper asked, "Norm?"

"That's his real name. He thought Norm wasn't cool enough."

Solemnly, the boy said, "Norman Jackson, that's my daddy." Then he asked, "What's wrong with your hand?"

Harper felt bold and said, "Where is he?"

"Workin' at the nursing home. He subs there."

The boy asked, "What's wrong with your hand?"

The woman said, "That's not polite."

Harper said, "It's okay." She looked the boy right in the eye. His eyes looked startlingly like Jack's. Bluer than blue. Like cat's eye marbles or an unpolluted sky. She said, "I was in a car accident."

The woman said, "That's awful."

"I'm almost over it."

"I know your aunt."

"Aunt Jill?"

"I worked for her some when I was in high school. I love the orchard. I love the blossoms. I love working with the illegals. They're mostly nice."

She got up and leaped over to a dresser and opened a stubborn drawer. She took out a framed photograph, and with her one free hand, she propped it up. A wedding photo. "Recognize us?"

"Of course."

"You're beautiful, Mama," the boy said.

"You're biased," she said. Then, to Harper she said: "You look a bit swimmy headed."

"I might be."

"I don't want to come off hard-hearted. But you know you're not the first and you won't be the last." Under her breath, she said: "He can't keep it where it belongs."

"Why…"

"Why do I put up with it?"

Harper worried about how much the boy was absorbing. Plenty, it seemed. She only nodded.

"I can't divorce him. I don't want to be the first wife who gets nada while he goes on to be famous."

"They're laws about that."

"Bless your heart. Those kind of laws don't apply to people like me." She tucked her breast back inside the dress. Then: "Listen, maybe you could help me some. I need to pack up these pictures and take 'em to the gallery in Morgantown. Norm's work sells lickety-split."

"You can't…"

"Oh, but I can. I do it all the time. You might could say it's our system. I need the money for these kids."

Without thinking, without considering, Harper did as she was told. Lulu brooked no dithering, it seemed. Before she knew it, they were on the interstate, headed to Morgantown. The mountains rose away, green, in full summer. Lulu turned on Sirius radio: a station that played meditative music. Harper had always derisively thought of that kind of music as lobotomy music, but Lulu said, "It's boring as fuck, but it keeps the kids calm." Sure enough, they both fell asleep in their car seats. A cookie dangled from one of Nathan's hands. The puppy fell asleep in Harper's sling.

Harper told her the story of the accident. The story of Doug. The story of who she was before. She got into it; she elaborated and said things she'd never said out loud. At one point, Lulu reached over and squeezed her hand, a zing, an electric charge. She whispered, "Jesus. You've been through a lot."

A big state mower was determinedly mowing down all the wildflowers alongside the highway. Lulu said, "I sure wish they wouldn't do that."

"Why?"

"The birds."

"The birds die?"

"No, silly. They need the cover."

They stopped at a drive-thru espresso shop, and Lulu bought them both lattes. She fished under her seat and brought out a round silver flask almost the size of a black-and-white cookie, and from that flask she poured a slug of coffee liqueur into each of their paper cups. "It's not Kahlua," she said. "It's the cheap stuff."

"Fine by me," Harper said.

"Sugar makes everything better," Lulu said. "Sugar and butter."

"Truer words were never spoken," Harper said, grinning.

They maneuvered into downtown Morgantown, parked, and Lulu said, "You won't mind stayin' out here with the kids, will you?"

"Uh, no."

"We'll go for Thai takeout after this. We can get the kids Happy Meals and eat in the McDonald's parking lot. Okay?"

"Sure."

Lulu unloaded the van, making every effort to move gingerly and treat the paintings with reverence. Mostly, Harper figured, she did not want to wake up the kids. She had never considered how much care goes into keeping kids asleep. She hadn't noticed before, but the floor of the van on the driver's side was thick with old leaves, brown, withered, curled up at the edges. While Lulu was inside, Harper checked her phone. There was one text from Jack. "Tomorrow night?" She let the text sit there. No answer seemed exactly right.

Jack's world, Norm's world, the world of bourbon and no tea kettle, the world of his ambition, the raw discomfort of sitting naked on his bed—all that seemed like an island she was leaving. Leaving for the mainland.

Smorgasbord

A bleak Thursday in February, it wasn't Claire's turn; she waited to slip stealthily through the house until the interloper and Rex had gone to bed and Pete was busy in the kitchen, with the odor of curry and yeast dough sailing down the sunroom hall. To relieve tension, Pete baked bread and cooked meals Claire had to admit were enticing. It was his regimen. On occasion she had come upon him, punching down the dough, a short tumbler of bourbon at the ready, country twang on Spotify free-associating for him, a smorgasbord of love-sorrow, Patsy Cline, and Willie Nelson. They hardly acknowledged each other those nights. Trying to keep it together was the primary practice in their reluctant hearts. He loved the interloper, his wife. Claire loved Rex. Claire imagined that Pete hoped—as she did for too long—that the sex part would wear itself out and Rex and the interloper would come to their senses. She always dreaded bumping into Pete. Rex's lover's husband. It's a mouthful, but precise. My husband's lover's husband.

 The house had been a refuge, with its leather furniture and floor-to-ceiling books. At this time of night, the solid house of her married life almost touched her fondly with its ordinariness. But not quite. Not quite. The rub of it, the interloper, the love-y sounds, the straining to hear the slightest giggle or thud of a headboard, and the straining *not* to hear it—Claire couldn't relax. Sometimes she downed two Benadryl with a Moscow mule to make it through the night.

She hadn't told Rex that once the semester ended, she might be living with her parents in Whistle Pig, a place she'd worked hard to escape. Tail between her legs, she was screwing up her courage to ask them if she could come home. Her father taught at a nearby college; her mother had made a career of volunteering. It wasn't the best solution, but it might be the start of a cure for what ailed her, her husband in love with another woman, her tenure case denied. When she was young, she had pictured herself swimming in a vast pool of choices, like the wide end of a funnel. Now at forty-six she was at the itty-bitty skinny end of the funnel. The ear worm *I don't want to be alone* governed her choices. That's why (or one reason why, she wanted to aim for God's honest truth here) she'd put up with The Situation, as she called it in therapy.

Her parents had a huge place, a model of deferred maintenance, a metaphor applicable to houses, bodies, cars, research projects, marriages, any relationship, really, when you got right down to it. Houses were cheap in Whistle Pig, especially big-family executive monstrosities abandoned once coal was finished, and the paper plant shut down. The vision of moving into their decrepit carriage house was a bit fuzzy. It slid away in her mind's eye, as if she were tipsy. She'd be close enough to her parents to ward off loneliness. Close enough to help, if they needed help. Close, but not under the same roof. Boundaries—that was it. She wanted unambiguous boundaries. "Good luck with that," her snarky therapist had said.

For almost two years, she had struggled to keep everyone in a Covid bubble—Rex, his lover, the lover's husband, and her stepdaughter Mia. Being that person, the cautious one, she felt prudish, self-conscious. She lay awake at night, trying to find the least offensive words to use—making herself small, speaking softly—to convince everyone to comply with her bubble parameters. Then Mia brought Cody into it. And adolescent Cody and Mia were not capable of persistent caution. Was anyone, anymore? She felt on the verge of chucking the entire project. To hell with it. Let's get Covid and get it over with. She was vaxxed. But so what? With the new variant running amok, she would have to negotiate a new Covid bubble with her parents who had adopted the laissez-faire attitude of some oldsters who thought they could "dance between the raindrops," as her mother liked to say, keeping fast to some rules, masking up for the grocery at seven in the morning, but meeting face-to-face with students in a windowless office on campus (her father) and doing tai-chi with friends indoors (her mother), all without masks. Her mother thought that she couldn't catch Covid from people she knew. Whenever Claire heard that, she envisioned an ugly little emoji. Ha!

Polyamory.
Sounds like something silky. The word slipped off Claire Wyman's tongue like a tentative French kiss. Smooth. Luxurious, like crème brûlée. Or a cashmere sweater.
But it wasn't. *It. Wasn't.*
In Anthro 201 she tended to gloss over sexual variations. There were always students titillated by the bonobos and the notion of using sex to solve conflicts. In spite of all the talk, ad nauseam, about consent, after class they would swipe each other's rear ends, grinning over their shoulders; in the spring, she would spy them under the oak trees on the quad, their hands under each other's T-shirts. She wouldn't admit it, but sexual variations creeped her out. She couldn't even rattle off what cultures approved of multiple sexual partners within marriage. Too many was one way of looking at that.
At the far precipice of consciousness, she was aware of the possibility of getting together with Pete. Plasticity dictated it,

and plasticity was one way *cultures* survived. Didn't marriage require plasticity, too? Polyamorous marriage, even more so. But—eek—he did not attract her in the least. An IT guy like Rex, he had spent his prolonged adolescence coding, his face glued to a computer screen. There was something moist in that face, as if he were about to break into a Sunday-jogger-sweat. When they had their little meetings to process their feelings—meetings called by Rex—Pete would take off his sandals or shoes and socks. His bare feet, soap-white, somehow raw, seemed obscene. She didn't want to get any closer to what she thought of as his flesh.

Small surefire comforts meant more to her now than she ever imagined they might. Nineteen Crimes wine. Music from her younger days. A closed living room door, where beside the fiery window of the wood stove, she would drink and attempt to read and love up the one dog left, before the hullaballoo of the forced-gregarious evenings. Much as she wanted to be one of those women with gratitude lists on Facebook, she couldn't be, not now. And reading took focus; she was short on focus. In the red, almost destitute, when it came to focus. How much focus, how much research, had gone into the purchase of the Vermont Castings stove. They had pored over brochures; they discussed the color as if it really mattered. Spending money was something that came along with married life. Now the shiny enamel Biscuit finish on the stove jeered at her. She would aim for ease, for consolation, but all roads led back to what they had become. She wanted to fling all the goddamn good silver from its walnut case onto the bamboo floor; she had the urge to deface art they had purchased together.

Mia—seventeen, a senior—was cat-sitting for two weeks at her aunt's condo in town, no doubt glad to get away from Rex, who tried to act neutral toward the interloper when Mia was at home, but Mia was a smart cookie. Since the interloper and Rex fell in love, Mia had sought out every excuse to be away from home. Cat-sitting was convenient. For several reasons. Cody was probably keeping her company—a euphemism for them fucking themselves weak in the knees. Claire would stop by. She would text first. She did not want to witness lust or love, whatever it was.

In her mind's eye, when she pictured herself driving away in the red Volvo, Mia was there in the passenger seat, her bare feet propped on the dash, her toenails painted the same color as the car, like candy apples. It was always summer, the windows rolled down, music they agreed on: Lucinda Williams, Lula Wiles. When Mia was younger, they had developed a mutual fantasy of a girls' road trip, beaches, working on their tans side by side, browsing in the quaint little towns along Lake Michigan, the shop windows full of sundresses and tie-dye. They would gorge themselves on takeout waffle fries for dinner if they wanted. How long the trip would last seemed vague. Sometimes they talked about getting jobs at an ice cream store or summer carnival. All pre-pandemic froth—The Before Times. And where was Rex in these daydreams? Neither Mia nor Claire wanted to bring him and his bossy ways into it. After years with Rex, Claire had adopted the habit of keeping quiet to forestall his problem-solving, rants, and bright ideas. With Mia, Claire talked a blue streak. They both did. Now Mia had Cody. And she was all set to start college in the fall, even if it went remote.

This particular night, Claire could have been grateful for wool socks if she weren't cynical. Maybe that was a gratitude list strategy: asking herself what she might have been grateful for if she were capable of it. She maneuvered into snow boots. She tugged on a wool hat. Just past the living room, Brandy whimpering brought her up sharp.

Brandy lay on a big dog bed, an LL Bean circle. Pete squatted beside her, concern stamped on his face, a seemingly permanent affect; although Claire sometimes wondered how hard he had to work to maintain it, she never asked, she never probed. A stained-glass lamp cast dollops of rainbow over the dog's matted coat. She was old.

"She's not feeling well," Pete whispered. This was one of his saving graces, a deep connection to animals.

Claire knelt on the squishy foam edge of the dog bed. A listless Brandy stared at her soulfully. *Do something.* The general consensus: Brandy was depressed; their other dog had died at the age of seventeen right after Christmas; Brandy searched for him, in the pantry, on the sun porch, in the fields. She was off her feed and refused even venison and salmon.

Pete said, "It's not depression."

"No?" Claire methodically massaged Brandy's right shoulder. She resented him thinking he knew Brandy all that well.

"Something's wrong." He pointed to her right flank. "If I touch her here, she flinches."

A ballad from the kitchen struck her as profoundly sad. She shrugged off her tote bag. Whispering, too, she said, "I'll stay with her. She can see Dr. Val in the morning."

Pete said, "You go. I'll look after her." They both massaged Brandy, the closest they had ever been. Brandy almost smiled.

Claire glanced sideways, into Pete's stony green eyes. She was near enough to smell the bourbon, and something else. Curry? Onions? She said, "That's okay."

"No, go."

Peeved, not wanting to show it, Claire asked, "Why?"

"I know you like to be out of the house . . ."

"Why're we whispering? Is there a beast we don't want to rouse?"

Without hesitation, Pete said, "That would be the beast with two backs."

And they laughed. A rueful laugh. A bark. Unduly loud. Survivors—strangers—in a lifeboat who have discovered the loss of some essential item.

All gentle business, Pete whispered, "I'll sleep on the sofa. No problem. I'll be right here if she gets worse. You go."

Then he touched her hand, a solid gesture of compassion, nothing more. He didn't want her either, not in the carnal sense. He said, "Where *do* you go?"

Sometimes when it wasn't her turn, Claire went to her office on campus and graded student work. She had managed that escape all winter, taking the four-wheel drive, negotiating the Midwestern snow piled in pyramids, orange from the streetlights, the darkness cushioned by it.

This frigid night she parked in front of Rex's sister's condo. The condos all had ornate porch lights, medieval looking, heavy iron. She texted Mia: *I'm out front. Need anything?* She waited, flicked on the car radio, listened to a fragment of a weather report. Mia texted back: *I feel punky.* Claire answered: *Punky?* While Claire wondered if that meant they didn't want to be interrupted, Mia kept typing: *Thx for stopping by. I'm ok. TTYS.* And she ended it with a kiss emoji. *Kiss-kiss,* Claire typed. When she drove away, she noticed Cody's Crown Vic parked at the corner. A teddy bear lay in the back window.

She had gotten used to life with Mia, this new period. Communicating almost solely via text messages. Mia driving. Mia having sex. Rex didn't like it. But Claire had convinced him that he could not stop her. So long as she kept her grades high, Claire campaigned for Mia's autonomy. Mia was seventeen, almost eighteen. She was in love, state of mind and body that made you crazy, as if drug-addled, according to Claire, but she kept that to herself.

She parked in a gravel lot near her building and dodged the students wandering campus like a murder of crows, the women dressed scantily, the men emitting irregular bursts of testosterone, shouting, merrily kicking things. She understood. They had to get out of the remote-learning cages, their dorm rooms. They had all been vaxxed. She usually enjoyed their unpredictable, explosive glee. Tonight she felt like their haggard mother, their frustrated neighbor, their heartsick big sister.

She unzipped her parka halfway and pulled up a mask that she kept attached to a beaded chain used for reading glasses by women with violet-tinted white hair. She thought this derisively, but the chain was convenient. Now I am among you, O white-haired women.

She let the students get ahead. They were bunching up periodically to staple posters on kiosks. She went up to one. *We Have the Right to Exist.* A white supremacy slogan. She took a picture of it and sent it to the Dean of Students, a man she had dated a long time ago when he was an assistant professor and she was a waitress at a high-end restaurant while working on her Ph.D. in Baltimore. Out here in the boonies of central Ohio, Baltimore seemed like life on another planet. She still had his cell phone number. He wouldn't want to hear from her. She suspected him and the president of baked-in willful ignorance of prejudice and discrimination on *their* campus. And they'd probably delete messages from her without opening them. Since her tenure decision had come down, they viewed her as an overnight malcontent. She might start a fire in the admin building after hours. She might carry a knife in her boot. A year ago, despite a Covid ban on gatherings of more than five people, students had mounted a campaign in support of her. For a week they camped out where the president had to walk past them every morning. Rabble-rouser and badass—that was her reputation now. She was neither, but who was it said that once your reputation is shot, you can live freely? More like invisibly.

At her office, she kept a pillow and a gray Army blanket in the file cabinet, and some nights, at a certain drowsy point, she might nap on the Navajo rug she and Rex had optimistically purchased on their honeymoon in New Mexico. Empty boxes scavenged from the copy room were stacked in one corner. She might have packed for half an hour. Books she wanted to keep. Knick-knacks she'd swiped from home, over time. A pitcher filled with fake hydrangeas. What had been the point of all that effort to make the office homey? Tears popped out when she thought of all the sciatica-inducing drudgery in her near future. She wasn't even sure that Rex would help. A futile train of thought. She grabbed two folders of student work and slammed out.

Her father might advise getting a grip, his favorite admonishment.

Through most of Covid, the only all-night espresso shop in town had stayed open for take-out. A public service. Now, post-vax, the owner insisted upon checking vax cards; the employees scoffed at it behind the owner's back. But Claire valued the ritual of flipping open her pink faux-leather case she had purchased for her vax card. Then she laid claim to a big table and scanned the news on her phone. Thanks to Rex and the interloper, she'd gained a modicum of skill at compartmentalizing: a minute of political reaction and musing was all she could spare. She tucked in her ear buds to wordless southwestern flute music and spread all the student papers out like a fence. The fence communicated: Don't bother me. If you were upset at your love life or the politicization of mask-wearing, you could feign a serious interest in grading. That was one good thing about teaching. You could lose yourself in it. You had to. Odious, labor-intensive, grading was always there to be done, like housework. The refrigerated glass case at the espresso shop was stacked with sweet treats, lemon bars and carrot cake and tiramisu. Every sweet from a happier time. She'd lived out her life at this espresso bar. The desserts shiny under glass beckoned to her and then they didn't. On a subliminal level, critical of herself, she had decided she didn't deserve dessert.

A white boy in a red watch cap popped into the cafe, accompanied by a Black girl bundled into a puffy ski jacket, her legs bare. Neither wore a mask. The boy had been a girl up until last September. Claire couldn't get past calling them girls and boys, to herself. When she addressed her classes, she said, "People!" And she was still catching on to asking for their preferred pronouns at the start of every semester.

The boy spotted her. She always felt that she had a stamp or tattoo on her forehead that read *I did not get tenure.* Translated, that meant she was unworthy, a fake, had wasted years of her life, did not deserve respect, and so on. But the boy was one of her faves. He took off his cap and bowed in her direction like a courtier, showing off for the girl more than for Claire. A charmer, he winked at her as if they were in cahoots. In that wink was everything they understood about each other. He had written an A paper, and she had emailed him to praise it. He had confided his desire to go to grad school.

What would her life consist of without moments like this? For the students, someone else would take her place, someone more cool, perhaps someone straight out of grad school, eager, brilliant. Maybe a person of color, and by peeling away from academe and making room for that POC, she will have done her bit to chip away at the public white space of Anthro. Maybe she could even stop thinking phrases like *public white space.*

Still, she would miss the students more than they might know.

That little tug—longing that had nothing to do with Rex, longing for the person she was when she first started teaching—that tug righted her course almost imperceptibly. She worked. For two hours. At midnight she packed up and steeled herself to face the weather. Heavy snow blew erratically outside the plate glass window. The barista had put on some reggae.

Maybe it was the music, the way it faded as the door closed, like a vacation she forgot to take, maybe it was the mental flash of Baltimore earlier. She went outside to the sting of snow and stared at the blurry moon. A woman in a ratty fur coat stood smoking on the balcony of the building. Thick-headed, Claire had disremembered Baltimore dreams of single women living in apartments above the shops in Fells Point, above a record store or bar.

She could live there. There, meaning alone.

The slog of disassembling her marriage was still ahead. She could see it now, like the inner workings of a machine. A machine she understood. It would be a clinical task, requiring lists and calling her mother and taking Brandy to the vet. She would buy those masks with the gussets that make a tight fit over your nose and under your chin. She would buy a digital thermometer and Covid tests to take wherever she went. She would be the woman with the Covid Kit. Someone optimistic.

Again, she turned her face up to the woman on the balcony, but she wasn't what Claire had perceived initially. The woman wasn't wearing a vintage fur coat. She wore a belted fleece bathrobe and with one hand she held it tight at her neck, as if that would keep her warm. She flung her cigarette stub over the balcony. "Goddamn snow," the woman growled, shaking a fist at the sky. It didn't matter. Scraps of rumination and experience had coalesced into something Claire could hold onto. The women in Baltimore had smoked on fire escapes. They soaked in tubs of lavender salts. Red birds reposed on their kimonos. Billie Holiday tunes hummed under their skin.

Sally's Tangent

The conference room in Hagerstown felt soulless and Gary thought, how fitting. He was glad to have spent the morning outdoors with his 10th graders, even if some of them had been ill-dressed for the weather and complained. Outdoors—among brassy fallen leaf debris and small critters—was where Gary felt most comfortable. His principal thought that the elective course—Literature and the Environment—was an excuse to tromp around outdoors and read Ed Abbey, and in this he was not entirely wrong.

Now, a robust nurse stood at the head of the corporate-length table where the couples found their seating and held hands. Outside, a neon Emergency sign glowed, and storm clouds—November bruisers—seemed to press against the mottled trunks of the sycamores. Gary and Sally had come in last and taken seats at the end of the table, near the door. He felt her knee against his, but not reassuringly, rather, she bumped him.

He surmised that, except for the nurse, Sally was the oldest woman in the room. Forty-one on her last birthday, a frozen day in March when snow had filled the crocuses. She had been a late bloomer, finishing college a decade before. Not long after that, even though they'd known each other for ages, they fell in love at a Friday afternoon happy hour meet-up in a bar, something they both felt sheepish about. The way they had used happy hour as a crutch. Supposedly everyone at the meet-up was interested in a river trip, but Gary did not hear any discussion of that. Now they never went to meet-ups or happy hour. Over time, the common denominator of their family unit, as Gary called it, was a lack of adventurousness. A shyness about uncertainty. No whitewater trips, no oral sex. They were more inclined to spend Friday afternoons at a hardware superstore, plotting some weekend project.

"Let's start with our feelings," the nurse chirped. "Just shout out whatever you're feeling, being here."

"Nervous."

"Apprehensive."

"Excited."

"Tense."

"Hopeful."

"Ditto."

The nurse cast an encouraging look their way. Sally said, "Resentful." Gary averted his gaze. There was a pause; he imagined everyone in the room interpreted—wrongly—what she'd said.

"I mean—"

Briskly, the nurse said, "We don't want to linger on explanations."

Sally tugged a ballpoint from her purse and wrote Gary a note on the back of the paper folder they'd been given. Her handwriting sprawled drunkenly on the pebbled surface of the folder. "It's easy for others," she wrote. Gary whispered in her ear. "I know." Peripherally, he could see her blinking away tears.

The IVF loan had come from Sally's mother and Wilson, who was to become her stepfather. Although Sally would never think of Wilson as a stepfather. She would only use that word when put in situations that demanded formality and roles and definition. Gary's high school teacher's health insurance would not pay for it. Sally worked in a garden center, tending plants, a seasonal job with minimal benefits. She could've been a high school teacher, too, but she had given it up after a year. The students had teased her unmercifully. She had come home dog-tired, furious, several times a week. The students had been cruel, pitiless. She had hated them in return, slamming books to the floor to gain their attention. Whatever history she might have taught flew out the window. For seven years she had worked at the nursery, and they had tried to get pregnant. She despised the expression everyone used: We're trying. She never used it in public, but others did. When she heard it, she pictured the nightly toil, the labor.

They did everything right and willingly. The birth control pills to make egg retrieval easier. The shots. The vaginal ultrasounds to measure the follicles of her ovaries. The retrieval. Gary with his flat sperm producing whatever he could into a plastic cup. The transfer of the three near-pristine embryos. The way that hurt. She had not expected it to hurt so much. All for nothing. She had bled them out. Four more had been frozen, and Gary said, "We'll try again."

Sally let it ride. She thought about going to talk to Jill Zebrak, who had, oddly, become her confidante, but she decided against it. She felt a bit ashamed of confiding in an old woman, a former employer, as if she didn't trust women her own age. And she didn't. She felt surrounded by baby bumps; it's what she noticed first about women. At night in bed, she cried, and the tears ran silently down her cheeks and into her hair. It hurt to know she was keeping it from him. She would drag herself to work, down time at the nursery, where all the equipment was being stored and the greenhouses scrubbed, where she had room to be honest with herself. Gary was caught up in the school term ending—finals, grades, a Christmas play. The juniors and seniors put on a winter dance, and Gary chaperoned the dance and the after-hours drug-and-drink-free party. She imagined him coming home around six in the morning, after breakfast at Denny's with the students, to find her gone. She hadn't taken many clothes. In the Bahamas she wouldn't need them.

I'm so so sorry, her note read. That wasn't completely true, or all of it, but she felt she had to take responsibility. To express what was true would've taken too long to get right, and she might have lost her resolve. She might have written: I have to leave my sorrow. I want to take pleasure in small things again. It hurt too much. I'm accepting my fate. I've decided that babies are not that important to me, after all. We can't live in a lab. Find someone fertile and try. All the beauty, if there was beauty, went out of it. Beauty—poof. I can't remember what we started with. I can't remember who I was. Or who I'm meant to be.

The tiny cement-block house had been her childhood vacation home, situated where the cay was a mere few hundred yards wide, with the warm aqua-green ocean not far from the front door and the deep cold harbor at the end of the dock behind the house. Every night after dinner, Sally's mother had made up a bed for her, a foam pad and a cushy sleeping bag, on a mahogany slab table salvaged from a ship. Where they ate their meals. Her mother had tried to convince her that a camp cot would be better and even then, an only child, Sally recognized her mother's subtext: you're a maverick, and stubborn. Sally had insisted on keeping the curly waves in view out the window should she wake up in the middle of the night. She pretended she was at sea. Her parents had slept in the one bedroom. They had been owners of an orchard near the Potomac River, in Maryland; Jill Zebrak had purchased it after Sally's father died. It made Sally blue to know that the blossoms and fruit belonged to someone else. While they were in high school and her parents still owned the orchard, she and Gary had met when they picked apples before school started in the fall. For years after that, when she drove by the apple trees, she imagined their younger selves, still deep in the trees, climbing ladders, stopping to banter inexpertly. All they knew of each other then was a programmed sense of wonder and boy-girl aversion left over from grade school.

Sally worked the orchard for one season after her mother sold it. All the girls who worked would gather on Jill's porch when the day was done. Behind her back, the girls called Jill Zebrak a witch, a crone, a bitch, as if to deflect the influence she had over them. She paid their wages; she dispensed occasional wisdom. Jill Zebrak lived alone and told them that she loved living alone. Or she would say, "I don't live alone. I have my dog." She provided iced tea and stale store-bought muffins for the girls. There was no reason for the boys not to show up, but they never did. That left the girls free to slide into more intimate discussions. At first it would start as joking, teasing. Then someone would say, So-and-so has a great ass. They would discuss the anatomy of the boys, sometimes cautiously, sometimes crudely. Jill Zebrak, lounging nearby in a wicker chair, never stopped them. In fact, it seemed as if they performed for her, testing her, to see if, like most adults, she would disapprove. Sally would clam up. Jill Zebrak noticed that and once, privately, she said to Sally, "It's all right, you know. Some people aren't that interested in it."

It. Doing it. Chemistry.

But I am, Sally silently protested. If she had agreed with Jill Zebrak that would have been the end of her life, for the pursuit of boys was paramount in the lives of all the girls except the lesbians. Lesbians were lucky, Sally thought then. Pursuing boys had felt like a part-time job, exhausting, awash in disappointment. Jill Zebrak knew that, knew it in her bones, yet Sally could not come over and be on her team. Her joyless celibate team.

When she was a girl on vacation with her parents, they had usually kept their bedroom door open, whispering to and fro with Sally, the room around her drenched in moonlight. You could smell saltwater and shrimp or bonefish, whatever they had eaten for dinner. She never tired of the sound of the honey-tongued sea. Her father sometimes had to stay behind to tend the orchard, but she and her mother had spent almost every school holiday on the cay, even summers, when the tropical air was soupy and the sand would burn your feet. Surrounded by water. They had somehow missed the hurricanes. Their place had always been spared. The Queen's Highway, a dusty path, led down to the village where you could buy bread and milk and gin and limes. Basics. No cars were allowed; that accounted for the pure air and water. Islanders toodled around in beige golf carts.

Since her father's death, her mother had rented the house out to vacationers. They called it the little house; her mother had built a bigger house farther away from the village, at the wide end of the cay, a house that might have fit into any suburb in the States, a gray cedar box with picture window views: a slice of sugar sand and the crisp sailboats. Her mother had met Wilson there and they were starting a business, a shop for tourists with money to burn, and they were about to marry. Wilson was from Northern Virginia; he had retired to the cay after years of public service, devising agricultural projects in developing nations. He exhibited the good cheer of a man for whom life had worked out. He was seventy, his investments had paid off, he jogged three times a week, and left his prescription packet of Viagra on the kitchen windowsill for all to notice.

Five months had passed since Sally took possession of the little house. She hadn't ventured farther away than Marsh Harbour, where she purchased groceries and saw Dr. Lieu, a therapist whose parents also lived nearby. They should have had a club for people who ended up in the Bahamas for their parents' sake.

Or you could get more specific than that, Petrucci always said. It could be a club for wild kids, now grown, whose fate it was to end up on a strait-laced dollop of sand, close but not close enough to decadent places like Barbados. A windsurfer and builder of websites for purveyors of Caribbean subcultures, Petrucci had come to help his parents construct their dream boat. The websites had titles like "How to Fake a Jamaican Patois" and "Cannabis Corner: Your Guide to Ganja." He had arrived lugging a large bottle of tequila, and on the ferry from Marsh Harbour, he and Sally had recognized each other as possible kindred souls. Petrucci was in his thirties, from Vermont. He wore his hair in dreads. Aside from his board, his most treasured possession was a framed photo of himself at Bob Marley's funeral in front of the Jamaican National Heroes Arena. Only ten years old, he'd gone with his father, a die-hard reggae fan. Petrucci had been to Nine Miles, where Bob grew up, a pilgrimage. Petrucci was capable of obsession, of abrupt changes in his life to follow imperious orders from within. He claimed to welcome such changes. To await them with curiosity.

Sally couldn't imagine why she had worked and lived in a northerly climate where it might snow on Mother's Day, and she couldn't imagine why she had been married. What makes a body choose the hard way? She was still married, but it was only a word, like female or Caucasian, a box you checked when called upon.

The tattered board games lay stacked under a window, Monopoly and Risk and Clue. The same shells and glass balls and starfish from her childhood were arranged on a high shelf above the mahogany table. The curtains hung limply, a calico print. She did not mind mess, domestic disorder. A lived-in feel. If she had a knack for anything, it was frugality. She did not like to buy new things. If the idea arose, she would wonder, Can't I make do? As if she wanted to grow old with all things having been used up or worn out. A good thing, her mother said, since you've little money. Sally would work in the shop to earn her keep, a decision her mother made, and Sally accepted as an opportunity that would prevent her turning completely uncivilized. Every day she would have to get up and face the public.

It was May, three days before her mother's wedding, right before the summer heat descended. A Saturday morning. She had taken a book and her coffee and a mango cut up in a bowl down to a lawn chair past the cement steps looking out to sea. Over the years, renters had left books at the house and there was an impressive library, a hodge-podge, from *Cooking with Conch* to *All the Pretty Horses* to *Thirty-Three Thorns*, a biography of St. Rose of Lima, what Sally had chosen from the shelf a few days ago. St. Rose of Lima was into pain, she had told Petrucci. Someone had fashioned a silver crown for her, with thirty-three thorns, one for each year Christ had been on earth. She had worn it under her habit, with the exquisite thorn tips pricking her skull. This behavior was so far on the opposite end of the spectrum from Sally's life that she read it the way you read sci-fi. Petrucci read only philosophy and New Age books, his own brand of torment. A thought she kept to herself. This morning, she could not concentrate on reading. Her mind felt assaulted from all sides, and all assaults were about Gary. Gary was on his way. He had called Wilson from Fort Lauderdale. He had said, "Tell her it's the impeded stream that sings. Wendell Berry. I'll bring the essay with me. It's about marriage." What she recalled about Wendell Berry would fit in a thimble. He refused to use a computer and farmed with horses. She had never read Wendell Berry; what she knew she knew because Gary had talked about him. Gary taught English at an alternative school for kids who had gotten caught in deviant acts—they were shoplifters or graffiti hooligans. Gary's mission was to reconnect them with the natural world.

The lawn chair had webbing missing, and its aluminum joints were gritty with sand. Her mother thought it was eccentric—and not endearingly so—that Sally would tolerate a worn-out beach chair or cheese from which she'd cut a moldy crust. Her clothes had a salty look. But she was happy. Happier. She had renounced pretense. From time to time, the woman orchardist—old Jill Zebrak—would float in her mind. Why wouldn't she leave her the fuck alone? She had become like her without intending to. At all. The bleached-out clothes, the quirky habits.

After breakfast she put on sandals and walked down the Queen's Highway toward the white house in the village where the shop was to be. Dust rolled like talcum between her toes. Sunlight broke through the palm trees. She wondered if Petrucci was about. Petrucci of the dreadlocks, the steel pan CDs. Petrucci, who wanted her. All the mile to the village, deliberately turning from thoughts of Gary, she pictured Petrucci and tentative wavelets of desire for Petrucci washed up in her body. She had never felt them before. It was only a matter of time. For months after leaving Gary, she thought she had come to the end of coupling. She would observe couples and recognize the stylized gestures and complicity—she had done that. She had loved Gary, as best she could. But when she left, she thought it would never happen again. Or so soon. It would hurt too much. Now she had to admit there was a vibe with Petrucci. A carnal look. His dewy brown eyes lassoing her female energy. Her nipples perked up. Come with me, we make our own decadence, he would say. Rock this place.

A brush in one hand, dripping with bright green paint, Wilson waved from the front porch of the shop. He was painting shutters. Her mother had gone on a buying jaunt, via mail boats and prop planes, to San Juan and Trinidad and islands in between. "She's found batik tablecloths," Wilson said. "She called."

Wilson was jolly, a flirt. He wore workmen's clothes, denim and chambray, with élan. His silver hair curled appealingly about his ears. He loved women and knew exactly when to empathize and how. All genuine, she thought. Dangerous. There was a look he tried out on her whenever her mother went into the kitchen or glanced away. Not penetrating, but annoying, as if he hadn't quite caught on to being almost married, although he had been married before, in his thirties, to a woman who had died in a plane crash.

"You want to paint or re-pot geraniums?"

"I'll paint," Sally said.

Wilson went inside and brought out his battered short-wave. He used the short-wave mainly to follow NOAA and all storms. For someone who had lived an intrepid life, he had an outsized fear of storms, but Sally did not. With her there, he turned to a talk radio station out of Boca Raton. They had their drill. They would listen to the news from around the world and speak their minds. This is what she did with Wilson. She had steadfastly refused to stay for dinner while her mother was away—going on two weeks.

Wilson was for current events, and her mother was for dissecting the lives of relatives and neighbors who lived in Maryland. Her mother always expected her to recall more about those people than she did. It felt like getting on a bus and eavesdropping on the gossip of strangers. Lately, they had found common interest in the shop, in the building of a business, not the inventory. Sally would look at the stock perplexedly, the hand-painted napkin rings made from tin cans, the gaudy jewelry. People from Maryland or Iowa or New Hampshire would buy them, and they would end up in a closet or at a church rummage sale.

She felt herself at the center of a wheel, with Wilson and her mother two spokes, and Petrucci another. Petrucci was for those wavelets of physicality, a new sensation she thought she could control. This getting what you need from different folks struck Sally as far superior to being married. It left her with seamless time of her own, time in which she would read or rave or lie besotted in a hammock watching the sunlight create aqueous patterns on the trees.

And what would besot her? Memories. Loneliness. But none of it was worth doing anything about. It was like weather. Dr. Lieu said, "Watch it all go by. "

"What's up with you?" Wilson asked.

She shook her hands beside her ears, a nervous gesture. "Just a wee bit jittery. About Gary."

Wilson laid an even stroke of the green paint on the shutter's edge. He glanced up. "He sounded all right."

"But what does he want?"

Chickens came ruffling around the corner of the house next door, cackles trembling in the air. Their feathers whiskey-colored. A boy went by whistling, on a bicycle.

"You would know more than I," Wilson said. He turned to her, his face frankly concerned. "Do you want to talk?"

Paint dripped onto his court shoe. She felt grateful that he was willing to get his shoes dirty, for her. But then she thought, addressing herself, Have you no dignity?

"It's okay. I'll be all right."

And she would. One thing life had revealed to her was this: She would be all right.

Petrucci came around the corner, toting a sign on his shoulder. He had painted the sign: Gail's Goodies. Lime-green letters twined among red geraniums in pink pots. Another thing he was good at, sign-painting. He and Wilson had that in common; they were good with their hands. It created camaraderie between them she could never share. It made her feel she wasn't really *good* at anything. When she thought this, a little voice would say, What about plants? What about all those delphiniums you grew from seed? But on the cay she hadn't lifted a finger to grow anything; she wanted nature to take its course.

"How's every little thing?" Petrucci asked. He set the sign against the porch wall. His voice was kind, something she forgot when he wasn't around.

"Nice sign," Wilson said, turning his back on them.

She could smell weed when Petrucci drew near, weed and the funky, waxy odor of his white man dreads. Sally did not like to consider what others thought of Petrucci. When she did, he came up short. He came up with parts missing. His interests were wind and reggae, intoxicants, and the writings of Ken Wilbur. She might meander down that discriminatory path a while and then realize that the criticisms she attributed to others were her own. What she repressed to have his company. And what did he repress to have hers? All of this was part of the unspoken courtship. What surely would have to come out later.

He smiled his charming smile and squeezed her hip, a gesture appetitive, proprietary. A yen for him sluiced through her, her pickiness chucked overboard.

In Marsh Harbour, Gary and Gail—Sally's mother—caught the same ferry, a launch with room for sixteen passengers. He felt an immediate allegiance to Gail; he patted the cushioned bench, and she smiled and sat down. He missed his own parents at that moment. Vagabonds, they moved from RV park to RV park, visiting their children and grandchildren in Memphis and Asheville. He hadn't seen them in over a year. He kept an eye on their house in Whistle Pig. Sometimes he went inside his old bedroom, which was like a time capsule, with a poster of The Talking Heads curling away from the wall and plastic golf trophies on the bookshelf. Why did his parents leave it the same? They were busy moving on was all he came up with. He wished he had their gift for moving on.

"You can watch everything from here," he said, knowing Gail would want to see her packages, six oversize cartons taped shut and tied up with yellow clothesline.

"The shop opens next week," she said.

"Wilson said as much." He turned around and watched the foamy V in the launch's wake. Sky, wind, water, all worked toward harmony, but he had seen the place in storms, the palm trees hammered low to the ground. Hurricane season started June 1st. By then, he wanted to be back home in Whistle Pig, with Sally. He imagined her jeans still hanging on a hook in their closet. Maybe they would start jogging together again. She had said he wasn't doing his share of the emotional work. He thought she was projecting. They would have to have one of those painful heart-to-heart talks; he relished the thought. Or told himself he did.

"Beautiful day," Gail declared.

That was one thing he remembered about her, her declarations, her certainty. She was convivial most of the time. Manners were important to her, a guiding principle. She might never be aloof or puzzling. Never slam doors. Never cry surreptitiously. He thought that, but then he wondered: How would she be different in a marriage? Marriage changed you. You went into it thinking it would settle old scores, patch up the old damage. If that didn't quite happen—and when did it?—you might revert to infantile behaviors. Even Gail, at seventy, might revert. You could never be privy to another marriage's miasma. Thank God.

Her tan was under control, not too dark. She wore a swervy straw hat, the color of toast. Brown and cream, her hair and makeup and clothes ranged through variations of those colors. Sunlight twinkled on her engagement diamond.

"Sunday's the big day?"

She smiled apologetically. "It's just a small ceremony. At the lighthouse."

She was making it small, fearful he might find a wedding dispiriting.

"I'm happy for you," Gary said. "I am."

She placed a bony matriarchal hand on his arm and leaned close enough to speak into his ear, over the engine's surge. "You know about Petrucci?"

"I know about Petrucci." Petrucci was one among many island personalities Sally had written about. What Gail said made him anxious, as if he might be seasick.

"Just so you know what to expect."

Yes, they had written letters—real letters, on paper, Sally's on green steno pages ripped from a tablet and his on school stationary. Using email had seemed to diminish the seriousness of their correspondence. He had examined the postmarks carefully and he had pictured her doing the same, like reading tea leaves. Once she'd placed the merest beginning of a fiddlehead fern into the envelope. A hibiscus petal. Her letters were like history lessons and character sketches. The island people, descended from British loyalists. The Black girl in the nylon dress, selling her auntie's key lime pie at a rickety wooden stand. He knew it was a sundown community and that the girl could not live on the island. How did Sally stand living there, knowing that?

"I don't want to give up easily." He wasn't sure why he said this, why he felt he had to put up a front to Gail now.

Her straw hat nearly blew off in the wind and she reared back to secure it, squeaking. "You still love her, then?"

"I still love her," he shouted into the wind. He thought of times he and Sally had ridden around the county in his pickup, maybe on the way to Lowe's, just goofing, laughing about nothing, and he would shout out the window, "I love *her*." Had that really been carefree? Or was there, underneath the manic display, fear? He couldn't be sure. After she left, he had not felt sure of much. He had stuttered over his own zip code. He had spent a month of evenings watching television shows he'd never watched before, ignoring slippery piles of essays that needed to be graded. He would get uncharacteristically pissed—ripping up clothes she'd left, shouting at the walls. Fuck you, fuck you, fuck you. His therapist said, Anger is a clear, unmistakable signal that you're in pain. No shit, Sherlock, his father used to say. He tried not to think about the frozen embryos.

The captain throttled her down; the launch puttered mutedly into the harbor; the white frame houses with the Day-Glo trim came closer and closer, as if brought into focus by a camera. Music accompanied their approach, drifting from an outdoor café, big band horns. He thought of dancing, that Sally was a good dancer.

Gail leaned toward him again. He smelled her perfume, a wintry spicy scent, and he thought, She needs a new perfume for her Bahamian life. "They don't bathe much," she said. "Petrucci and Sally." Then he remembered that she loved to gossip. That didn't jibe with her attention to manners—it was the dark side of manners. Structure versus no-holds-barred information sharing. Her cheeks colored at what she'd said, a red glow that didn't suit her monochromatic scheme. "I don't think they've—you know—yet."

"I don't care," he said. That was a lie and he knew it. His birthday was in April and when he went to renew his driver's license, he had eavesdropped on a conversation between two clerks at the license bureau. One woman asked, "You still with James?" "James's gone," the other woman said. "You know me—my nerves can't stand one man for too long." Something had clicked into place: the conviction that Sally would find someone else before he would. Women could do that. He needed to see her before she let go. He had skipped graduation. A family emergency, he told the principal.

"I hope you can straighten her out," Gail said. Then, with its own grace, the launch settled into the dock like the hips of a big-boned woman.

Wilson and Sally were waiting beside a fish stand, thatched with grasses, where a bare-chested local wielded a knife on a just-caught fish the color of blue steel. Sally smiled tentatively; she wore an old apple red T-shirt from the orchard where they had worked years ago. He took her hand and kissed her cheek. Her hand trembled. "You're here," she said. "You're here."

Weather shifted, wind and a squall. Gary was the only one bothered by it. He shivered and said, "Hurricane season's not for a few weeks, right?"

Sally laughed that off. A nervous laugh with a cynical edge to it. A laugh that dismissed him, but he shoved away that thought.

She used to have a nickname for his penis. She hadn't thought of it in a long time, but it was on the tip of her tongue. Fully clothed, gin-and-tonics at hand, they lounged on the bed in the rosy tinge of sunset, a place she was surprised to find herself. Ocean breezes cut through the louvered windows. She could touch him; he was her *husband*. That meant that she could reach out and touch him. He had grown a mustache; it looked good on him. There was a map of his body in her mind, on her fingertips.

He wanted her more than he had since the first year. She was tanned and freckled and lean. She hadn't shaved her legs, and the hair curled in a sweet mat from the knees down, bleached frosty from the sun. He took her hand.

His hand felt dry and cool and expert. The feel of his fingers against hers—simply fingers—called in all her nerve endings: pay attention! She drank in his smell, reminiscent of their home, the yellow teapot, the Shasta daisies, his soccer ball in the corner of the foyer. He raised her hand to his mouth and kissed the palm of her hand. He kissed her wrist. The rosy tinge had bled away, and the room was near-dark. When she moaned that little come-and-get-me moan, he thought, Now we're getting somewhere. He had never heard her moan like that.

What they did was about them, not making babies. It was adoration, of a sort. Religious in the pagan sense. Sally gave herself up to it. She worked up a good sweat. See, see, she said to the old orchardist, I'm not like you. I do want it. Sometimes.

In a while, she felt herself plucked from the after-drowse by the urge to pee. The bathroom seemed garish, too brightly lit. A place to shower and take care of bodily functions. It felt almost like an outdoor bathhouse; the cement blocks had not been covered over with paneling. There was a small round shaving mirror above the sink, the mirror her father had used decades before. On the wooden plank shelf, she kept shampoo, conditioner, an unscented lotion, and a froufrou vanilla candle, given to her by her mother. The candle had not been lit. She hadn't even removed the cellophane wrapping. When she opened the door into the bedroom, Gary wasn't there.

She slipped into a robe and sighed against the front doorframe, giving her eyes time to adjust to the dark. She spied him in his boxers down at the concrete steps, a blocky flat figure, standing as if to call to someone. She knew him well enough: He would be caught up in awe, astonished. She never quite felt that the way he did. Beasts of doubt stripped it from her. Two stars were visible. The palm leaves made a sound like delicate knives being sharpened. The sea splashed and the birds cooed. It was all of one piece: birds, water, night, the after-sex feel exhilarating, melancholy. What did it mean that they had done it?

Then she saw Petrucci and the moon rising. Petrucci on his sailboard tacked southwesterly, a silver element of nature against the moon. Some deviance, a hardness of heart, a counter-flux at once shocking and familiar, came over her. Stormy weather, Dr. Lieu. She rummaged in a closet and found her sleeping bag and laid it atop a yoga mat on the mahogany slab. From there she would be able to see Petrucci's flight and Gary on the steps or Gary in bed when he came in. It was a perfect triangle. A release of the tension of a straight line. She might talk with Gary after he went to bed, the way she had talked to her parents when she was a girl, aiming her stage-whisper toward the bedroom door, with the glass balls rescued from the deep shining above her on a shelf. She might say, What about the frozen babies? She might say, What song *is* sung by the impeded stream? It would all take time to figure out.

Years later, when the cay was in the path of a Cat 5, Sally thought, "That wasn't an innocent reunion beside the fish monger." Not really, because she had been full of herself. Attached to outcome, Petrucci would have said. But that wasn't true. She was attached to the unpredictability. Bad storms. The grip of sex like the flu. The Cat 5 was after Wilson died, after her mother had moved to Cape May. Sally evacuated to New Orleans, where she got a job landscaping year-round. Gary worked at an environmental camp in one of the state parks near Whistle Pig. A good soul, he wanted to live with his parents who were old now, making a go of aging-in-place. When the Cat 5 hit, he didn't call to see if she was all right. Petrucci had fled to Jamaica.

In New Orleans she retrieved adolescent dreams of living alone. After work, she paid more attention to her clothes and preferred menswear, black cigarette pants and white shirts. In one hand, she'd carry a bloody mary down the scuzzy street. She wore bold sunglasses. Frenchman seems to be where unusual things happened. One chilly night outside The Spotted Cat, a man smoking a cigarette whispered, "You look beautiful." She thinks that doesn't matter anymore. But his remark rolled over and over in her mind for a few days, like a winning lottery ticket worth two dollars or five. Hardly worth cashing in.

Pivot

GT Diggs is a trained journalist he's fond of saying on a night out, when we're on the bulletproof slope of tequila. By that he means: my whole existence might seem rinky-dink, a dying enterprise, but it's not. He's the publisher at The Linden Gem, a thrice-weekly newspaper that still serves remote Appalachian counties. The Gem was founded in the early 20th century by his great-grandfather. So, history. Family money. Legacy that's frayed around the edges. GT is addicted to cable news and more podcasts than I ever imagined existed. He knows the word pivot is overused, but it's right there on the tip of his tongue when revealing his own who, what, where, when, why.

We went to high school together. Here in Linden Mines. He returned before I did. I lived in New Orleans for nineteen years and came home to Linden Mines when my guy and I broke up and my hurricane anxiety peaked. I rented a narrow downtown storefront, built in 1854, its windows murky with grime, the interior thick with dust that might have been there since the Civil War. I scrubbed it slick as bone, replaced the filthy toilet, and moved in two massage tables along with all my professional gear. I am a healer and a secret keeper. I know every density of muscle, every possible knot concealed. The sign out front reads: Comfort Zone.

GT and I usually catch up at the club, in a motley circle of people we knew back when. Until today. Until he showed up for his first massage.

In the last few minutes, I have discovered that he has a pink scar on his left knee from banging into a rock when he was dumped out of a raft on the Nantahala. I know that he wears plaid boxers. The soles of his feet are sensitive—he's ticklish there. His sketchy intake form admits only to seasonal allergies.

GT's pivot was visited upon him—his words—during the pandemic, but after vaxes.

Before Lisa died in Africa. Before his nephew Chris was sent out west to a private school for wayward kids. Before his sister gave up the Linden Gem to move away with her new man, an economics professor. Before his niece Nicole dropped out of Vanderbilt and went on the road with a punk band. Before his mother's dementia set in and they had to move her to an affordable memory care unit. Before he and Deuce bought the hardware store that had been empty since Home Depot came in. They turned it into an eclectic music club that draws people from as far away as Pittsburgh and Baltimore. They kept the faded blue name emblazoned above the double doors: Linden Mines Hardware.

Sometimes I think I need a map with pushpins to keep track of his whereabouts when he was a young man. Tuscaloosa. Little Rock. Memphis. Chicago. I knew all these things. We have sat around a teetering table at the club, drinking too much, with those old acquaintances, trying out this and that, searching for common threads, when whatever band he has hired takes a break. At the club, his history emerges in asides and tidy stories intended to manage the narrative. Although people in this crew have sheepishly revealed what they might regret the next sober morning. Shy discussions of sex. Humiliations as a child.

Now, here he is lying face-up on a table in my massage studio, the light pearly-dim, bergamot scent in a diffuser, music like a lullaby, and GT Diggs excavates, inch by inch, while I pull at his trapezius muscles and knead his shoulders. I want blood flowing into his heart, literally, metaphorically. I want to ask: Why now? Why do I get the unabridged version on this gusty fall day?

Chicago, 2022. With Lisa in Africa, with him in his own little universe. He did things his way, for the most part. When he was able to figure out what that meant. He and Lisa had been together for nine years, since grad school in Tuscaloosa—so what was his way and what was her way had blurred. He had his superstitions, akin to avoiding cracks on the Linden Mines sidewalk when he was a boy. Give a wide berth to black cats. Never leave a rocking chair rocking. And so on.

"These are my two drops of rain," he says, "going down the windowpane. All the best and all the worst come from which of them is first." All the worst had already happened; he had a hard time believing in the best.

GT has a theory about time. It's like balancing while skateboarding—his passion when he was too young to drive. You can be in the present and still contain the future and past, hope and melancholy, as well as the faceless clock of the eternal cosmic. You had to. It's all about staying awake. "I thought I was awake," he says. I work my way down an arm adorned with a Sun Studio tattoo, the vintage mic and stylized sun rays evoking nostalgia for something I never knew. One thing he missed in Lisa's absence was the sound of his own voice practicing endearments. Saying, "I got this," when she was stressed. But talking to himself felt old-mannish and had lost its succor.

Balancing time was about waiting and not waiting. I have known waiting and not waiting, for GT. I have kept my own counsel, without a rag of hope that he would desire me the way I used to desire him.

It's true that GT and I went to high school together, but that doesn't mean we were friends. Even in a small town like Linden Mines there are class distinctions. I was an orchard rat. A kid working side by side with my parents, when there was work. His grandfather was a county commissioner, a country gentleman with property. GT wore the mantle of down-home wealth. An invisible cloak. He was surrounded by boys and girls who wore the right clothes with nonchalance. They spoke so readily of going to university. If they ever came close to trouble, there was someone to bail them out. We didn't know each other then. I knew *of* him; he did not know I existed. I didn't hold a grudge about that. It's just the way things were.

Now, decades later, he's come to me with secrets, like so many in Linden Mines and all the out-of-the-way hamlets and crossroad towns in name only since the mines and the paper mill and the tire factory dried up. I don't charge much even though I'm board certified. I am better at stockpiling the aborted dreams of my clients than I am at staring down my own.

He says, "Back then, in Chicago, even though Lisa was away indefinitely, a promise was a promise." He was going nowhere; he was the steady one, the reliable one. He was entrenched; wild horses couldn't budge him from their apartment near Wrigley Field. He wanted Lisa home; she would come home from South Africa when she was ready, when the Chicago weather turned to her liking. They had promised each other that they would never move to Linden Mines or anywhere near it. Too much baked-in cruelty and boredom, Lisa always cautioned if it came up.

Without Lisa, his appearance went awry, unkempt; he sometimes forgot to comb his fine hair, and it stuck up— hat hair—above his forehead. Before Chicago, when they still lived down South behind the Magnolia Curtain, in the halcyon days of impromptu trips to the Gulf and pitchers of margaritas on Sunday afternoon, he had bleached the tips of his hair nearly white, and it had made him feel free of his upbringing—I'm a guy who can play with his hair. That all seemed like youthful naivete. It made him cringe to think about it. But even after Lisa left, he shaved every other day; he didn't want to see the early gray in his beard. If he thought about actors he might resemble (a game he and Lisa once played on a road trip), he wasn't all that happy with the answer: A young Robert Duvall. Curmudgeonly, persnickety.

With two harmonicas laid out on a towel, and the rest in a Café du Monde coffee can at his feet, "Anybody Seen My Girl" seemed like a good place to start. The muted wail broke like a wave against the tiled bathroom wall.

A silence fell between us.

I imagined that he saw Lisa there, under the shower, her back to him, her hands pressed against the tiles, in the wet slap-slap of sex. Burn it up, he might have told himself. By *it* I think he would mean memories, double-edged swords.

He repeated what his Mama likes to say: "Time is a balm that heals us round the clock." She had said plenty when they told her they were pregnant and not getting married.

When they first moved in together, Lisa had scolded him: "That slimy coffee tin reminds me of them spittoons. Geezers sitting outside a ratty hotel. I'm a talking to you. You play that filthy mouth harp in the bathroom." She liked to say that she was from an itty-bitty town in Alabama where they were so poor that the architecture students from Auburn showed up and built houses for the people out of straw bales and scavenged corrugated tin. What philosopher said that we don't shed our earlier selves, they merely nest within us? Lisa had worked hard to eradicate backwater Alabama from her voice and diction. Except with him. Except for the occasional dip like snuff into who she had been. Them spittoons. "Except for times when she was tipsy or frisky," he says. I wonder, what did she moan? *GT, honey, god*—.

They had met at an outdoor music festival, down by the Black Warrior River. She wore a sundress with flimsy straps tied in bows on her shoulders. There was a tiny black mole, like a pencil mark, in the fatty place between her arm and her breast. That place on a woman's body had always seemed sexual to him, vulnerable. He knows that I know bodies and that talk of bodies is not off-limits. The way she ate honeydew seduced him. She laid out a red-and-white checkerboard napkin on a bleacher; she cut the honeydew into crescents and scraped out what she called the innards; with the shiny blade of a Swiss Army knife, she delicately portioned each crescent into chunks that could be bitten from the rind. It had seemed efficient, elegant. The music had been of another time: Bessie Smith covers. She had seen him watching her and she offered him a crescent.

But when he told this story to his good friend Deuce Tate, Deuce said, Just an ordinary day in the kingdom of honeydew. Boy, you sure can tell you're not married.

How so? he had asked.

Numero uno, Deuce said, she'd have come back by now.

Before GT's pivot, Lisa had been volunteering for three weeks with vervet monkeys. Her village north of Johannesburg was eight hours ahead of Chicago time. The middle of the night. Almost Saturday. The volunteers slept in canvas yurts; an unceasing hiss and chirp, guttural barks and coughs and groans—birds and animals—surrounded the yurts in the night that she said was like flocked wallpaper. You remember that old-fashioned flocked wallpaper your mama has in the front bedroom? It's like that. A night with texture.

"I kept the time zones straight," GT says. It would be three in the morning, and in four hours she would get up and catch her ride into the village and email him. They didn't have Wi-Fi at the vervet station. She did not want a video chat via WhatsApp. She didn't want to text. But she hadn't said so. He just knew. She was on the other side of the world, and she wanted to feel it, the distance. To test it.

He dumped take-out paella into a bowl, set it in the wave, and punched in the number. Before the fridge he deliberated and picked out a Strong Bow cider and opened it and took a good long draw. At the coffee table, he laid out a cloth napkin and a fork, dimmed the sconces, and thought about what a heathen he had been until he met Lisa. She's the one who had told him he was grown-up and shouldn't eat chips straight out of the bag.

When his meal was ready, a thick wedge of ciabatta buttered to go along, he clicked on the remote and, as he ate, watched a special on Comedy Central. Did everyone have a family worthy of stand-up? Or were some things too grim? GT resented it when a comic made you laugh at something awful.

His degree was in journalism but the work he did—handyman this and that—was learned from a young age, alongside an uncle. The next day, he would finish tiling a dog bathing station for the couple near The Vic. They had three robust Dalmatians and wanted fire engine red tile. Fine by him, but he felt obligated to point out that buyers, should they ever sell, might have an aversion to red. Oh, they would never sell, the woman said. There are those who believe they will never sell, never get divorced, never run short of the accoutrements of comfort, and their children will never die before their eyes. It was a job that might take three hours of what the Chicago weather woman declared would be a sweet Saturday, with temps in the fifties. Then what?

If Lisa were at home, they might bundle up and power walk—her words—along the lake in the high bright mid-day sun. Ignoring or trying to ignore the sleek surge of traffic on Lakeshore Drive. Sometimes she trotted nimbly ahead of him, her thick flaxen ponytail swaying; sometimes an unspeakable anger would visit her; he saw it in her eyes and the precise way she moved, taking care not to touch him, not to lean into him inadvertently, not to pat his thigh, kiss his cheek—impulses she also had. This anger having to do with the baby was a holy terror. When that happened, he had waited it out.

The moment his phone rang, an old-fashioned business-like ring, he woke up cloudy headed from a nap he hadn't intended to take. The TV was on; he had cued up a movie but fallen asleep instead. His mouth tasted spoiled, tangy, from the shrimp boil residue in the paella. It took time to find the phone, time to wonder: What's wrong?

Now nothing's wrong, his big sister Nancy said.

At the sound of her voice—her gravelly lilt, deliberately charming—he mentally summoned up the mezzanine of the newspaper office. As editor-in-chief, her office. The typewriter collection—Olivettis and Smith-Coronas and one Smith Premier from the 1800's their granddad had purchased at an estate sale. The smell of carbon paper, crumbling newsprint, whiskey, and Balkan-Sobranie pipe tobacco: all smells he associated with his granddad, who had died when GT was five years old. The mezzanine like a vault of souvenirs, locked up and seldom entered, except for Nancy. Sort of the way he viewed the bedroom—he had slept on the sofa for two months and in his mind the bedroom was now an archive of their former life. Lisa had slept on the futon in the study.

Nancy had not changed a thing, had not made the mezzanine hers. She feared that if she purged the mezzanine of their granddad's things, she might not want to do the job anymore, she'd told GT. It's like he's there, his goddamned thumb in my back. She had her laptop, and he imagined that in a drawer she kept a vial of Shalimar and a flask of liquor.

She sped through her initial bulletins. It's already hotter than the hinges of hell. Mama's gone downstate. She took the alligator. I'm still at work.

The alligator. Their signal that their mother would gamble long hours at the casino. He could picture it: a red alligator-skin satchel. I had seen his mama leaving home with the big purse, a sneaky gleam in her eye. He turned on a light and made out the time. 10:10. It's kind of late. For work, he told her.

Tonight's Pride prom. The first in Linden Mines. He tells it to me in such detail; he has the words inscribed like newsprint on his mind.

GT whistled a long, astonished note. By that he meant: So, time has not stood still in Linden Mines.

I do not question this. I focus on his outer thigh.

Nancy scolded: Don't be judgmental.

You are.

Honey—I live here.

There was a pause, in which he imagined his sister took a sip of whatever her intoxicant of choice was that night. She was probably lonely, and GT's heart went out to her. He missed her, missed their youthful catapult toward a subterranean existence. The gin they drank surreptitiously. The night rides out to dive bars in the country. The fake IDs. Things were either *real* or *not real*. A fake ID was real. Sitting in their mama's Mustang was real—at three in the chilly morning out in the driveway, talking and sobering up. Their Rule for Life was this: The places where people tell you not to go are precisely the places you need to go.

He told her about the job he was on; he told her about Lisa's last email. He cleaned up as he talked. With one hand he rinsed his plate under running water. He rinsed the cider bottle and nestled it in the recycling bin. Wind battered the bay window that looked over their street. The roofs of cars appeared slick, jewel-like—it had rained.

He knew his mama wasn't all right to drive. He knew that she crept down Highway 40 to the casino at 45 miles an hour.

You can't tell her a damn thing, Nancy said. You can't tell her the sun rises in the east. I know you want us to take away her license, but do you have any idea how hard that would be?

That would be hard.

Chris didn't go, she said, regretfully, as if she could have corrected that, if she'd wanted to.

Why not?

He's straight as they come. And shy.

He had another call—Deuce—and he told Nancy he wanted to take the call. She said she would stay on hold. Deuce wanted him to come to a club in the neighborhood where any kind of music might be on tap— blues, zydeco, hip-hop, country. That might fill up the time until Lisa emailed.

Lisa emailing him was the bright spot, the Main Event. Nothing else mattered. When she first left, he had tried to imagine what it would be like to be single again. He had Googled an old girlfriend and found out that she had advertised for a used kayak, that she worked for a congressman in Birmingham. He had bought a few new shirts. But after three wasted nights of such drivel—what ifs—he saw his life without Lisa for what it was. By that he meant that he was not in charge. And still, he believed that what he waited for was worth something. That those years were worth something. Worth conserving.

When he got back to his sister, he said, I'm meeting Deuce, even though she knew Deuce and did not trust him. They had gone to school together for a couple years.

You go, she said. Call me later.

Righteous Times had the funk. It was a club free of a dedicated genre and the owners wanted you to know that upfront. There was a tattered 8 x 11-inch American flag in one window, a burn from Iraqi explosives marring the field of stars. Signed photos of Miranda Lambert and Dolly. Two dueling, upright pianos, scarred and cigarette-burned over decades. Christmas lights blinked. Commemorative plates hung over an aluminum coat rack like you'd find in a church basement. Martin Luther King, Bobby Kennedy, Obama. The wooden floor shook when late-nighters got up to dance, and mellifluous Black voices laid down memories or longing. Or it might be some zydeco band passing through town, and the tables had to be pushed back for riotous two-steppers. If you closed your eyes, you might think you could smell crawfish cooking.

Sometimes he caught himself longing for memories he knew he did not have the right to. He wouldn't mind seeing the prom-goers in their costumes and finery. Or drinking with Nancy at the Gem. You had to stay home to have the right to certain memories. By home he meant Linden Mines, a town that time forgot. But how could you appreciate it if you never had a yardstick by which to measure? This was a familiar refrain.

All I ever said was: I appreciate it. I had taken my leave and gone to New Orleans after my certification. I wasn't ignorant of the wider world like some people in Linden Mines. And he would say: Fee, you might fly the coop again someday. He was the only one who called me Fee. Most people called me Fiona. And to my grandmother, born in Wicklow, I'm Fiona Maeve Brenders. You see, GT, I have my own family history, worth savoring.

He says, "When I got there, Deuce was on stage, singing 'Members Only.'" The house blues band at Righteous Times almost always invited Deuce up to sing. He had wormed his way into their inner circle by driving one of the Chicago Blues tour buses that once a year shuttled for an evening between clubs: Hothouse to Checkerboard to Lee's Unleaded all the way to Wallace's Catfish Corner.

He says, "I could imagine the Pride prom."

Would they segregate themselves according to gender proclivities? What he knew about the LGBTQ crowd could fit in a teacup, but that didn't keep him from wishing them well. Nicole had proclaimed herself bi and taught him to say, "LGBTQIA," but he always had to catch his breath before the IA and seldom managed it.

Deuce sat down and swiped the hair from his forehead. He slapped the table GT had claimed. "Good to see you." He was still in his work clothes, herringbone slacks and a white shirt that glowed like the moon.

GT laughed for no reason. Deuce always made him feel there were still adventures to be had. Deuce drank beer and GT drank a Dr. Pepper. They talked about the ungodly weather, the waiting for Lisa's email.

Since they lost the baby, Deuce had made every effort to be solicitous and kind. He cradled his beer bottle in both hands, gave GT a studied look of pure empathy, and said, I hope everything with Lees works out in your favor. The phone in GT's pants pocket vibrated and he pulled it out to see who might be calling.

He left his jacket and his Dr. Pepper and went outside under the flapping awning, which was skimpy and did not shelter him from the slanting drizzle. Chris had sent a video, and it took him a moment to figure that out. The screen was orange, grainy, and below the orange was a message from Chris: Pride's on fire.

He called Chris, and all he can remember is Chris saying, No one's made it out the front. A few are getting out the back. And: I wish you could *see* it, Uncle GT. He said it was at the Maple Hotel. And Maple Hotel, Maple Hotel, kept flashing in GT's thoughts. He doesn't remember hanging up.

Now he says: "We used to go there to party. It was abandoned then. You remember, right?"

But I never partied with GT. I sometimes lurked near an alley as he and his friends turboed away from his mama's house. My teenage years can be characterized as lurking; my grade school years, I read novels on the steps during recess.

GT's shirt was chilled, damp. He went back inside; the music was a monotonous, harsh version of "Back Door Man." Murder and sex—he wasn't up for it. He made his excuses to Deuce; his heart raced, getting back to the apartment. He missed Lisa then, big-time. He wanted to hear from her, and he didn't want to think about going to Linden Mines. The Maple Hotel had sprawled in decay at what used to be the edge of town, tucked in a mishmash of trees that must be over one hundred years old. He could recall a high school debauch or two there, in the ruins, his ass eaten up with mosquito bites.

He wanted his niece safe and sound in her prom get-up. Nicole. An almost seventeen-year-old girl who played the saxophone and sent him postcards from her travels, signed with hearts and Xs for kisses. She had spent last summer in Sweden, growing up. When she came home, she wanted to be called Nick, but he hadn't gotten used to it.

Lisa's email was waiting. The subject line: Change of plans

GT—
I want to stay another couple weeks. I'm going out to Zanzibar with another volunteer. She knows a great beach. I want to rinse the monkey poop out of my soul and get a good tan. Pongwe Beach if you want to look it up. We'll fly to Dar es Salaam and then Zanzibar. I just like saying Zanzibar. Yr girl—Lees

That was all.

His restless mind held two contrasting images. Lisa on a beach. Nicole possibly injured. He itched to do something. As if he'd conjured Nicole, just as he re-set the thermostat to sixty, Nancy texted: Chris told you about the fire. Nicole's alive but she's hurt bad.

I ask him to turn over. He's agile and does this deftly. I squirt more almond oil on my hands. GT says: "I needed to tell you all this. It's okay?"

"It's okay," I say. But is it? How will knowing all this change me, change him?

Until the baby was born, GT had not spent much time in hospitals. His granddad had died at home, of lung cancer. His father had died of a heart attack, driving back from Cumberland where he'd gone to play poker. His pickup had rocked into a field, hit a tree. I noted that we have gambling in our blood. Before my mother's Parkinson's left her home-bound, she would visit the casino, usually after Sunday church. She had the idea that gambling in her Sunday best made the trip to the casino semi-respectable. Lover of detail, GT says, "What was her Sunday best?"

"Kitten heels. Huge earrings. Necklaces that draped over her bodice."

He steers us back to hospitals. He's been in a few emergency rooms with friends who had gotten into minor altercations—nothing serious. When the baby—Joshua—was born, and put immediately into the NICU, they had begun six weeks of hospital living. There was a reassuring institutional smell about it—something abrasive, like a cleanser, and alcohol. And cotton. He had worn the blue papery caps and blue smocks. The nurses had been kind. Their kindness made Lisa weep.

After driving all night, he stood before West Penn hospital, our nearest Burn Unit. He was hungry, but he hadn't wanted to take the time for a full-blown breakfast, instead surviving on doughnuts and Red Bull over the long incision Interstates 80 and 90 make across the Rust Belt. The sky above Pittsburgh was soupy, cast with silver and pink to the east. He wore a tropical shirt and shorts, knowing he was driving into an early summer heatwave.

Nicole had always liked his tropical shirts. He reminded her of Jimmy Buffett. Once he and Nancy had taken the kids to see Jimmy Buffett. Nicole had been ten, Chris seven. That had been a very good day that he would not mind repeating.

Inside, a woman in Steelers scrubs directed him to Nicole's room. She reached in her pocket and handed him a fresh mask. Nancy met him in the hallway. In jeans and a wrinkled white linen shirt that she wore like a tunic—he knew, from years of hearing her talk about it—to disguise her thighs and rear end. Like a uniform. Her glasses were crusty with rhinestones. Her hair was still red, rich, thick, a nimbus, around her flat, pale face, and he smelled the scent of it—something vanilla-like—when he hugged her, held her. He had always thought she was beautiful. Now her eyes were swollen, raw from crying.

He whispered, How is she?

It's. Pretty. Bad. She inhaled sharply and held him at arm's length. But. She'll live. Three kids died.

Jesus. His head ached like unruly dogs let loose; he had the urge to slam his fist into the wall; on the drive east, he had banged the dashboard until he bruised the heel of one hand.

His sister shook her head and patted his back. Come see her. She's out but come see her. He pushed open the wide door. Nicole's arms and shoulders and chest were bandaged, her face exposed and dark red. She had lost some hair; he thought he could smell burnt hair.

He and Nancy spoke softly; Nicole opened her eyes at the sound of his voice.

Her voice slurring, wispy, drugged, she said, You don't look so hot.

GT tried to grin. What about you, kiddo?

My-new-look, she said, each word like a brick she was placing on a long wall she had only begun to build.

The ache to hold Nicole was palpable. But they weren't allowed.

A thick, glinting needle had been taped to the back of her hand, an intravenous drip. Her eyes swept shut. Her lashes were gone.

Back out in the hallway, Nancy told him what the doctors said. It would take weeks in the Burn Recovery Center. She would need surgery, skin grafts. There was a real danger of infection. As she talked, he walked her away from the room, toward the elevator. He had his arm around her waist. It felt good to touch and be touched. The hospital cues made him imagine he might see Lisa come around any corner.

What can I do?

I need you to look in on the Gem.

I haven't written a lede graf in years.

It's like riding a bicycle.

I don't know how long I can stay. The implication being: I *can* stay.

When's Lisa coming back?

It's not about that. Now was not the time to say *Zanzibar*. He wanted to say, It's about vowing that my ground time at home will always be brief. But Nicole suffering blotted out his truth.

"You called it home," I say, kneading one calf.

Nancy said, You've never been a good liar. Can we see where we are in ten days? Can we do that? She kissed his whiskery cheek. You can stay at my place. Mama's there, looking after Chris. Her phone squeaked and she took it out of her pocket and glanced at it. I'm pretty sure it was arson.

Jesus fuck.

What an inheritance. The Gem, his nephew, his mother, and Linden Mines. But there was Nancy, a fair assumption in her eyes: he was family, they needed him. When he and Lisa had been living the hospital life with the baby in the NICU, Nancy had come to Chicago the week before Christmas. She had run errands and done laundry. She had prepared meals they came home to, dead-tired. She had provided drinks to loosen their tongues, and they poured out their hearts to her night after night. One frosty Saturday evening, after Lisa had fallen asleep, he and Nancy had walked around to Righteous Times, but there was a padlock on the door. Still, it had felt good to get out. Nancy had said of Lisa, I see what it is about her. Why you love her. That was one time when GT cried.

The elevator opened; two male nurses with identical thin mustaches got off, talking about the NBA finals. One thing he knew for sure was that he was no longer in his own little universe of twelve hours ago. He had no rules of safety, no sidewalk cracks to avoid. He extrapolated forward—Nicole's life would never be the same. Three kids had died in a Pride prom fire. What would be the fallout from that? It hit him what a linchpin Nancy was, what a slender margin of energy she operated on, if she had to rely on him. If there were no one else she could depend on. I can handle it, he improvised.

In the pale blue interior of the elevator, what had been the marrow of his days and nights dried up—the dying baby little more than the size of a kitten in her arms, their sleeping arrangements, Lisa on the other side of the world—and he felt lighter, streamlined, curiously emancipated for a change.

Our time has been up for at least twelve minutes. I want to be enthralled by him now; I was when I was seventeen. But nothing's like seventeen. Have I broken ethical protocols? The room is still dim and smells like massage oil. The music has subsided. I rest one palm on GT's upper back. Through the gauzy curtains, I keep an eye on the parking lot just beyond the window. It's after four on a blustery day, with fog beginning to ease itself around town. The old woman from the orchard pulls up in her pickup. She likes to simply appear and ask me to fit her in. I usually do.

GT says, "Thanks." We both know he means too many things to name, years, the tequila, the physical healing, the story, no-judgement. His hands curl near his thighs.

The summer between grades eleven and twelve, we both worked at the orchard on Brick Mountain for a few weeks. My fantasies about him started there. I had imagined somehow ending up in the barn with him. In total privacy. I was so crazy-alive with hormones. I wanted him to be in charge. To reach around and pull me to him. His boner—a word I'd overheard a boy use, a word I couldn't get out of my head at that time—would be apparent. Would make me unsteady, quivering.

He's said so much, a gift of sorts. I absorbed it all. But now, standing there, my hands warm and oily, waiting for the old woman to ring the back doorbell, his story like a legend, larger than life, crowds me. Will there be room for his story inside me? Now, every time he grins and fake punches my arm, will I think: Lisa, the dying baby, honeydew, Lisa naked in the shower?

If I were to ever be invited into his sister's home where he still lives, would there be a display of photos of Lisa? Her electric bike leaning against the wall because he can't bear to give it away? A dreamcatcher she made at camp years ago? Will it be a museum devoted to Lisa?

I reach down and squeeze one of his hands. He squeezes back.

Kokoro

Old friends Alex Novak and Maria Bednar had reached the stage in life when they could say, without irony, "back in the day." Those four words could conjure riding the streetcar with Maria's uncle, the conductor, who always had a stash of Goetze's caramels in his jacket pocket, eating cod cakes—coddies—on Friday when only fish was allowed, the sluggish church festivals when the men of the parish went behind closed doors for gambling, and later, the Boone's Farm she and Maria drank when they allowed boys into Alex's basement lair.

Maria hadn't mentioned the fog. Or the potential for mini pileups. It was early March. Maria lived in Whistle Pig, and Alex had never been to Whistle Pig, or Bumfuck, as she called it to herself. Alex had drawn the short straw among Maria's old friends in Baltimore; she needed a change of scenery, and she could cheerfully follow dog care routines. She'd been laid off from an upscale doggy daycare in a former tobacco warehouse, not far from the old neighborhood. She came home smelling like dog fur, but she'd gotten used to it. It smelled a little like popcorn. Maria had told Alex the roads might get slick at 1500 feet, around the ramp that would take her into town and past Denny's and Lucky Liquors. She had said, "Stop and pick up some wine, would you?" But, as usual with Maria, it wasn't a request, but rather her assumption that what she wanted, she would get. She had cancer. She had had cancer off and on all her life. Under those circumstances, people give you leeway.

Alex had asked, "Are you…drinking?"

And Maria said, "Absolutely not. I just want to have it around."

Sure enough, two devil-may-care vehicles had taken the hairpin ramp too fast, and they had bounced off the guardrail and crashed into each other. Alex stopped to see if everyone was okay. They stood around, stamping their feet, their breath as gray as the cottony fog, waiting for a state trooper. One of them had a thermos and she poured espresso into paper cups for each of them. It was around five in the evening; their headlights glared every which way. The man wore a suit, and his long beard was either Amish or hipster. He had his phone out and expertly thumbed through messages, and he was driving a car—so not Amish, maybe. The woman with the thermos was dressed like the finest baby dyke, they used to call them, back when Alex fancied being a baby dyke. (Later she learned to live with being bi, and now she's learning to be celibate.) The woman wore a black leather jacket snug to her body. Heavy, cute, black boots. Thick short hair like Rachel Maddow. Glasses with chunky red frames. Stylish. Not someone Alex would expect to find in Whistle Pig, a forlorn corner of Appalachia. "I can move my truck," she said to Alex. So, the white truck was hers. The words HAPPY TRAILS APPLES were displayed on the driver's side door, along with a shiny red apple decal the size of a basketball.

"I think I can squeeze by," Alex said.

They said they were okay.

Alex eased on into town and stopped at Lucky Liquors where the clerk was at the glass door about to lock up. "After you," he said, "no one's comin' in tonight. Anybody smart'll be tucked up at home." She bought two bottles of Malbec and a pint of bourbon to keep in the car. Maria could get snotty on hard liquor and Alex had no guarantee she wouldn't fall off the wagon. When she started her car, she couldn't help but notice the clerk letting in two more customers, college girls they looked like, in short skirts and puffy coats, their long hair whipping in the wind, their cheeks rosy, cigarettes pinched tight and smoldering. Alex sat there a minute and spied on him insisting that they put out their cigarettes in an empty bottle. They were giggling all over each other, probably tipsy already. Or high. She remembered those days. Sort of. Alex and Maria had lived through much of their blurry teens and twenties together.

Now they were in their sixties.

Whatever good was going to happen to them had happened.

Maria liked to quote Ram Dass: We're just walking each other home.

At the end of a winding driveway, the house was a long, brick, mid-century modern rancher, encircled by a high black chain-link fence to keep the dogs in and the deer and bears out. Every light inside was ablaze, the windows and sliding glass doors amber blocks that made Alex long momentarily for quilting, a fantasy she had nurtured for years. She had a short list of crafty fantasies: embroidery, watercolors, knitting. Her mother was usually her excuse. The dogs were outside and put up a ferocious racket. There were four of them, all rescues. Alex knew them from Maria's Facebook posts. Blind Maudie. Teddy, a bear-like black mix of some kind, about eighty pounds. A shepherd who resembled a wolf. Called HB for Honeybun. And a scrappy three-legged mutt, part Chihuahua, part Corgi—Taffy. Her ears were long, her puppy eyes immediately appealing. These were Alex's charges. She'd agreed to take care of them while Maria was in Morgantown for surgery.

Maria had spoken of death freely. She'd been near death already. Several times. She always rallied, took on the bloom of mild good health, traveled to the southwest to see her son. She would purchase new notebooks and pens and start writing what she called her lyricals, small, tidy essays she would place in small magazines. Maria had a bias against attempts to monetize art. Such biases are a luxury, but Alex never said that. Alex wouldn't call any of those times complete recuperations; Maria did have body parts missing; but she liked to say that she wasn't ready to shuffle off this mortal coil. She worried about the dogs. There had been some talk of re-homing them before the surgery, but she couldn't bring herself to do it.

Alex sat in the dark car, the engine running for the heat, Annie Lennox playing, the bottle of bourbon open. She sipped from it, not scared, but anxious. The bourbon tugged at a seam of regret or apprehension. They hadn't seen each other since before the pandemic. What was she doing there?

She expected Maria to come out or, at the very least, open the door and corral the dogs. But a man with a fussy graying man-bun opened the side door, then a gate—there was an elaborate system of fences and gates. He curtly commanded the dogs inside. Then he invited Alex in. He smelled of weed and some kind of sweetish liquor. She didn't find it unpleasant. He seemed deliberately laid-back, trying too hard, in a shirt embroidered with cranes and woolen clogs on his feet. He relieved her of her duffel bag and the wine. A wave of heat unfurled around her body, inside her jacket, against her face. "I'm her cousin. Ezra," he said.

She remembered him, but he did not remember her. In fact, they had slept together that one time at the house Maria had rented in the seventies, above a deep green lake. The house with the steep driveway and a barn with a basketball court inside. Abandoned chicken coops. Dog shit in frozen piles. You had to shout to find other people in the house—it was that big. Certain rooms remained unfinished. In Alex's experience that was typical of the sort of people attracted to communal living. They were people too bewitched with erotic opportunities to tend to anything so prosaic as raising chickens or pruning an orchard or drywalling a dining room. Any old mattress would do.

The golden kitchen smelled of fish. Maria was a goddess in the steam of a chowder she was pulling together from scratch, a long wooden spoon in hand, her hair still thick, flying, as she balanced up and down on her toes, swishing, always moving, dancing. Laughing. Manic, Alex would call it. Upcoming surgery makes some people manic. Maria had a gritty black mark on her forehead; Ezra did, too.

She touched the mark and said, "Ash Wednesday."

"Oh, of course," Alex said. She couldn't remember the last time she'd gone to an Ash Wednesday service.

Alex yearned to steal away with her and talk. But there was Ezra to contend with. With a start, she realized how little time she spent in the company of men. Under the same roof. She resisted it. He said, "We need to put the bread in to warm. Where's the foil, timing was never your strong suit." Alex had expected Maria and Maria only. When they were alone, she'd ask her why Ezra was here when it was still four days until the surgery.

"Take her downstairs to the—voila—guest space," Maria said.

Ezra grabbed her exploding duffel bag, flicked on a light at the top of the basement stairs, and led her down. She had the sense of being guided by golden light. The stairs were honey-colored and the walls were butter yellow. An enormous oil painting of Hank Williams hung at the bottom of the stairs in an anteroom. Ezra opened the door to her room and flicked on more lights, and she was pleased. Maria had indeed created a wonderful space. She could picture sitting on the sofa later, with Maria. She'd explain everything then.

But it didn't happen that way. The rowdy dogs were outside, after several trips in and out. Alex saw that she would have to learn how to communicate individually with each one. Ezra and Alex drank the Malbec with dinner. Exhausted from the drive, she dozed off at the table after one bowl of chowder. She came to with them cleaning up the dishes. She got a second wind. She still wanted to connect with Maria, the way they had long ago. But Ezra wanted to playfully bait her and lord over her, bringing up foolish things Maria had said or done when they lived with six other people in the unfinished house. She laughed everything off. "You just want to control our history," she said.

He had a punishing attitude sometimes; other times he affected a meek bow with his hands together as if in supplication or accord. It was an affectation Alex detested; she was surprised that Maria put up with it.

Then Maria "started in," as Ezra called it. Possessed by electric energy, she cleaned out the fridge, divesting it of old bags of flour—milled from ancient grains that she hadn't gotten around to using up. Since the early days of the pandemic when most people were shut-ins, she had baked bread every two weeks and delivered it to her neighbors. She tossed out half-pints of moldy jam she'd made last summer and charcuterie meats that had turned leathery around the edges. She filled an entire gray rubber trash bin.

An old feeling came over Alex, part disgust, part envy, that Maria could afford to throw away so much. People with money buy more than they need: Alex's mother had told her this, about Maria's family. Her demented mother still had a sly way of denigrating Maria. She had done so all their lives.

They moved down a wide hall and Maria took all her bed linens and towels out of a closet, carried them into her bedroom, and threw them emphatically on the bed. She methodically folded each item. She opened a drawer and grabbed panties that were pale and tossed them in a small aluminum trash can. She kept only her black underwear. If she died on the operating table, she didn't want anyone to see those stains in her washed-out pastel briefs. After she died, she didn't want to be embarrassed about her underwear. She laughed ruefully when she realized what she'd said.

Alex started to say, "You're not going to die on the operating table," but it seemed phony, akin to a funeral-goer saying of someone who had died, "She's in a better place now." You just don't know.

Maria stopped her purge and stared out a window, into the country dark. It might have been midnight. But it was only a little after eight. "Come here," she said. She put her arms around Alex's waist. "This's gorgeous in the summer and fall. You can't see it right now. I planted a row of lilacs at the far fence. I planted a Rose of Sharon. Hollyhocks. Peonies. You'll see."

But how would Alex see? Her mother was never far from mind. A neighbor was looking in on her, but Alex thought: the gas stove, the water turn-off valve that her mother could never find in an emergency, the street where all sorts of danger lurks if you're ninety-one and don't have your wits about you.

She extricated herself from Maria's embrace. To soften that withdrawal, she tucked Maria's long hair behind one ear. Times of tenderness between them rose up. At the communal house, in the gloaming, they used to crawl into bed together, with wine in jelly glasses, and an open window beside the bed where curtains Maria had made herself would sail above them. The curtains were white with tiny star-like embellishments. That was the purest affection they knew. By purest Alex meant the least manipulative, the least transactional. "You want me to come back in the summer?"

Maria's skin was sallow and dry now. She kept reaching for a wart-like growth under her chin. It wasn't all that visible, but under her breath, she said, "This drives me batty."

She had been a beauty. "Maybe," she said, unconvincingly. "Maybe we'll both see summer."

Ezra was in the living room, switching between PBS and MSNBC. In a stage-whisper, Maria confided that he'd lost his hearing but refused to consider a hearing aid. Ezra and Maria had both been lucky with money, but she blew hers. She had spent money on trips she and Alex had taken, treating her to birding in Costa Rica several years in a row, a spa in Arizona, a New Zealand summer, and Andalusian villages one Christmas. They had started with equal generous inheritances from their grandfather. Ezra invested his in Apple and Nvidia. Alex tried to attribute identity markers to him, dredged from the past, to understand why he was here. As well as being considered rich in their family, he was a news junkie and a traveler. Once he had painstakingly explained to Alex the difference between being a tourist or a traveler. Whenever he returned from a few months out of the country, he repeated what he'd taken on, like a chameleon. Right now, he was so enamored with Japan that he talked about opening a Japanese lifestyle store. Kokoro, he'd call it. Heart. All details must merge with heart. Or arise from heart. She understood that he was still processing how to talk about his trip to Japan. He sounded like a Subaru commercial. Alex could recall his constant news updates when they lived in the communal house. No tidbit was too slight. He had done a deep dive into Elvis's death, playing the Madison Square Garden album over and over. It felt strange that they had been intimate. The idea of being intimate with anyone felt strange to her now.

They heard him letting in the canines, and they snuffled and boiled down the hall and Maria lay half-down on the bed and the dogs threw themselves at her. She was lost to Alex while she was relating to the dogs. It was like watching the mother of four toddlers. The dogs could always end a conversation. Alex thought: No one hugs me with abandon anymore. She had a brief pity party over that. Then she used the bathroom and went down to her golden room, its walkout sliding door, its patio adorned with yellow pots and shriveled geraniums, the bed Maria had made up with striped linen sheets. Alex had begun to feel proprietorial about it.

They had to get through three days before Ezra would drive Maria to Morgantown for the surgery. They'd spend the night there, in a hotel downtown, and she'd go into the hospital around six the next morning. Ezra would stay there. Alex would stay in Whistle Pig and take care of the dogs. It was a skeletal plan. All we need, Maria said, for now. She had typed out three pages of instructions for the dogs.

Maria had been sober for years, after all their carousing. For a while her ex had lived over the Knights of Columbus on Whistle Pig's Main Street. Homesick for her, he moved there to be nearby, in case she needed him. That's how Maria explained it to Alex. She insisted they file for divorce if they were going to live in the same town. She wanted to fall in love again and his presence would hamper that endeavor—the town was that small. Everyone went to the same music venue on Saturday nightm and to the same Film Club movies at the retro theater. Intoxication had been a hard habit to break. Maria's ex would drive her to the marijuana dispensary in the next town, and she stocked up on gummies that helped her make it through the night. The ex was gone now. He'd passed away a year before Alex's visit, in his sleep. Not from Covid, thank God, Maria had written when she made the announcement. Now she said that when she died, she wanted to micro-dose LSD; she wanted a transparent experience, apparently ignoring for a moment that once she died, there would be nothing left to lyricize, no dogs returning her devotion, no bread to bake with specialty flours, no birds to elicit delight. The micro-dose would supply a peak experience, a Last Peak Experience. Her pronunciation of those three words called for capital letters. She had made elaborate wake plans for her son and friends and neighbors, a playlist, a visual tribute, certain foods. Make it a wild party, she said, a real doozie.

They'd had their wild times. Wild times started when they were girls, living across the street from each other in Baltimore. They made their first communions together, grinning slyly in the confession line, as if they had the inside track to sins they didn't know the names of. One street could make a difference, in privilege, income, and expectations. Maria's family seemed wealthy to Alex. She divined this by observing at a very early age that their house had canvas awnings on the windows and air conditioning inside. Also, Maria's mother always wore prim flowered shirts tucked into her slacks. If they sat near each other at the eleven o'clock Mass, her father would slide a concealed amount, an envelope printed with his name, into the collection basket, while Alex dropped in the fifty cents her father had given her before she left the house. Maria's family vacationed in the Poconos, at Deep Creek Lake, in Nashville. They went out to eat. Alex's family would get take-out pizza. She clocked these differences.

Still, she didn't want to be Maria. There were too many rules at her house, along with a vial of the Blessed Mother's tears on a shelf above the sink.

After high school they went their separate ways.

A Catholic college in Pennsylvania awarded Alex a scholarship. Maria moved to College Park where she worked sporadically on a degree in horticulture. It wasn't her fault that her studies were sporadic; that's when her bouts with cancer began. She inherited the money, dropped out of school, and rented the big, unfinished communal house with the basketball court in the barn. Alex came for a weekend and stayed for a year, often waking up in emotional havoc next to someone she didn't know, her skin raw from the gin and black beauties she'd consumed. Ezra was one of those men. Anything worth doing is worth doing in excess—that was their motto.

When the lease was up, Alex went back to Baltimore and Maria joined a cult that spirited her away to a higher altitude, a town at 3000 feet, isolated, beat down by long winters. The cult leader, Mother Hannah, a woman in her fifties, used Maria up financially and sexually. Mother Hannah had wormed her way into local politics to make her real estate side hustle easier; Alex wished she had a dollar for every time she heard Mother Hannah's name. Sometimes she held the phone away from her ear; she was sick of it. When Maria managed to break free, Mother Hannah awarded her a tidy sum and made her sign a non-disclosure agreement. Maria escaped with another cultist, a man from Northern Ireland whose family cared for a butterfly conservancy on their former estate. She spent years flying hither and yon with him, gathering butterfly-friendly plants. This all took decades; they kept in touch with late-night phone calls, and later, email dispatches. Sometimes Alex didn't respond. But she needed her; Maria was a thin thread connecting her to the person she'd been before, a person with possibilities. And she didn't feel at home with the person she'd become. A lapsed Catholic. Twice divorced. A laid-off LPN. Living in the old Baltimore neighborhood in a walk-up apartment that reeked of squalor, with her demented mother who did not know her name.

The next morning, they went for a walk around Maria's neighborhood. Out of the blue Maria said, "Let's go in here. There's a meeting I need to pop into." Alex thought it would be AA. They were in the polished concrete basement of a church. The faint odor of incense emanated from upstairs. This was an ad hoc group of sick and elderly people who were composing their end-of-life documents. Sort of like a book club. Or a writing group. Abandoned cups of coffee—pale as green bean juice—surrounded a big cardboard container of garish pastries. This group had been ongoing for months. They had developed bonds that had to do with their imminent deaths and the freedom to discuss everything that crossed their minds about dying. They compared notes on whether they wanted funerals or memorial services later, in some tavern or outdoors when the weather might be more hospitable. They brought their laptops and streamed potential music for their memorials and funerals. They brought boxes of photos—these were to be broadcast on a monitor during the funerals and memorials. It may have been the most creative pursuit they had ever experienced.

It hit Alex: They were claiming the illusion of control. One wanted a movie shown at her memorial—*Love, Actually*. She wanted popcorn served. One wanted the music of Enya. Another, a bluesy version of "Just a Closer Walk with Thee." Another, Little Richard. Maria said that they enacted these funerals and memorial services and after the enactments they would giggle at their own pride in what they had created. But afterward, Maria was bitter. She was the youngest. She was convinced she would be the first among them to die.

Later, Alex was going on about this in her imagination, a sideline. The petty drama took place that night, after Maria and the dogs went to bed. Ezra and Alex drank and talked. They moved to the sofa, at either end. Ezra got up once to close the blinds. With his back to her, he said, "Lexie. You're Lexie." It was the first time he'd said her name. A version of her name.

"Yes?"

He came back to the sofa and stretched an arm along the back of it, a position that, from her experience, almost always indicated a possible seduction. "I remember you now," he said. "You look different now."

"Very observant," she said. "This is me forty years later. Back then I had rings on my fingers and bells on my toes. Your perfect hippie chick."

"Sorry. Did I offend you?"

"Not really," she said. Then: "I'm just done."

She got up and went downstairs. Her room had lost some of its glimmer. But claiming her solitude felt like ownership, of what she wasn't sure.

In the nest of fine linens, Alex catalogued what she wished she'd done differently. One of her favorite themes. She ought to have been more considerate of Maria. To have comforted her. In another time she might have put her arms generously around her and caressed her hair which used to lie silkily over her back just begging for touch. She might have squeezed her close for emphasis, meaning, we're in this together or I am here for you. For the first time in this portion of our lives, I am here for you. She could have apologized for all the times she ignored emails. She could have been more cordial to Ezra. He brought up feelings of embarrassment, cringe, and sadness, wishing she'd taken better care of herself with men. As if that mattered now. Yet, this seemed like her last resort. When her mother died, she might move here, to Whistle Pig. She might start a whole new life, among the hollyhocks.

They were like a miniature family of origin. Maria and Ezra, the parents. Alex, the wayward child. Maria liked to chatter about moving. She perused real estate ads in remote corners of the United States and Canada. She could get happily excited and then eventually agitated, as she compared locales and regions and granite counters versus soapstone counters. Her agitation came from knowing she was not capable of another move. Sometimes when she started down this road, Ezra would reach over and casually move breakable objects out of her range—a butter dish, glistening with soft butter, a half-finished bottle of wine, her pasta bowl. He told

Alex privately that Maria had slung a few heavy objects to the floor after meals. He worried the dogs would get slivers in their paws.

The next afternoon, Alex stole away with Maria's expensive binoculars; she went down to the creek nearby, ostensibly to watch birds. Some of the snow had melted and fingerlings of daffodil shoots had come up. Maria's property bordered an untended park, and a branch-tangled path along the creek led down into the park. She hoped for sunlight, but the circles of pine trees shut out most of the light. There was a green glow. She would gradually feel contented, she told herself, stopping to learn the names of various plants, using an app on her phone. She wished she could identify birds by their sounds, but that was a skill she hadn't learned and probably wouldn't. Some things are like that. She tried not to be mean to herself because she couldn't recognize bird sounds. She would take pride in things she did know. Snowdrops. Cyclamen. Sycamores.

She kept lists at night. Her short-term memory was slipping. Keeping lists gave her a sense of control, however Swiss-cheesy. Around dusk she noticed the cold and headed back. There were neighbors on faraway lots and that surprised her. Until then, her solo walk in the semi-dark, she hadn't noticed twinkling lights along the fences that bordered Maria's. She found the lights soothing, welcoming.

Then she dragged her heels. Nervous about whatever fresh uncertainty might await her. She didn't want to go in. Feverishly, she told herself: You. Could. Just. Leave. This seemed brilliant.

At the house she unlocked her car and left the hatchback open. She set a box of books on the ground. She'd been intending to drop them at Goodwill. The sliding door that led to her golden basement room was unlocked. Ever so quietly, she wadded up her clothes and crammed them into the duffel. She unplugged her devices and packed all that away, cords, tablet, Kindle, laptop. The dogs rumbled upstairs. She took her belongings to the car and stashed everything in the hatchback. Stars careened above her. So many stars. In Baltimore she rarely saw stars. She took a deep breath and struggled over whether to say goodbye. She would probably never see them again. One of those neighbors, the beneficiaries of Maria's sourdough, could take care of the dogs.

She wasn't far from the deck and a view of the living room; the French doors were closed. Maria knelt on the sofa, her long straight hair behind her. Her arms undulated, as if she were dancing. Van Morrison played on a turntable, and the sound came to Alex mutedly through the glass. Ezra knelt in front of her. Alex happened to be in the exact spot that gave her a near-perfect view of what came next. If she were a true friend, she'd have turned around and walked away. Ezra unbuttoned Maria's turquoise tunic. It was a watery color, like sea glass. He opened her tunic. She still had beautiful breasts. When he reached out and touched one and she shuddered with pleasure, Alex turned back toward the car.

Taffy, her little rescue heart full, had somehow escaped the fence. She jumped on the box of books and into the hatchback and over into the rear seat. Alex stealthily went inside and scooped up a jar of peanut butter, a saucer, a spoon, and when she got back to the car, Taffy was scrabbling after something in the brush. Alex smeared peanut butter on the saucer. She set it on the passenger seat. She grabbed Taffy like a piglet and plopped her down next to the peanut butter. "You're Kokoro from now on," she whispered. "Kokoro." The dog wasted no time switching her attention to the peanut butter. All doors shut, seat belt latched, with only the yellow fog lights on, they crept out the sinuous driveway to the main road. They were going somewhere.

Acknowledgments

Some of the stories in this collection were originally published in the following journals: *Pembroke Magazine, South Dakota Review,* and *Willow Springs*. I'm grateful to the editors of those journals.

I owe a debt of gratitude to Cornerstone Press, especially publisher Dr. Ross Tangedal. I'm also thankful for Paige Biever and her team of copy editors who worked with me patiently. Many thanks also to Sam Bjork and Sophie McPherson, the marketing staff at Cornerstone, and to Caitlin Hamilton Summie, publicist extraordinaire.

A squad of friends, readers and writers, read early drafts of these stories, and their comments and questions were enormously helpful. I will list them here, and hope that I haven't left anyone out. Laurie Scolefield, Kirsten Sundberg Lunstrum, Kristen Millares Young, Barbara Hurd, Matt Burgess, Jerry Gabriel, and Rob Davidson.

Thanks to my dear brother Dave who took me to the casino. Thanks to firefighter Gary Clutter who years ago explained river rescue in winter. Thanks to Tara Robisch who shared her IVF experience.

PATRICIA HENLEY is the author of three novels, five collections of stories, two chapbooks of poetry, and a stage play. Her first novel, *Hummingbird House*, was a finalist for the National Book Award and *The New Yorker* Fiction Prize. Haywire Books published a 20th Anniversary Edition of *Hummingbird House* in November 2019. Her short fiction has appeared in *The Atlantic, Ploughshares, The Boston Globe Sunday Magazine*, and other journals. Her first collection of stories, *Friday Night at Silver Star*, won the Montana First Book Award. Her work has been anthologized in *Best American Short Stories, The Pushcart Prize Anthology, Circle of Women, The Last Best Place*, and other anthologies. Her play *If I Hold My Tongue* premiered in September 2015, as part of the DC Women's Voices Theater Festival.

For 26 years she taught in the MFA Program in Creative Writing at Purdue University. She teaches a monthly Zoom workshop for women writers and lives in Kingston, Washington.

www.ingramcontent.com/pod-product-compliance
Lightning Source LLC
LaVergne TN
LVHW040058080526
838202LV00045B/3698